FALL WITH ME

SIXTH STREET BANDS #2

JAYNE FROST

SIXTH STREET PRESS

Edited by: Patricia D. Eddy — The Novel Fixer
Proofreading: Proofing With Style
Cover Design: Pink Ink Designs
Cover Photo: Period Images

SIXTH STREET
HISTORIC DISTRICT
6TH STREET PRESS
CONTEMPORARY ROMANCE

Nana

I miss you everyday. Thank you for everything.
I love you.

JOIN THE TOUR

Sign up for the Jayne's *Sixth Street Team* for the opportunity to receive **Pre-Release Review Copies** of the newest Sixth Street Bands Romances, exclusive content, and members only swag.

>>>http://bit.ly/2ykNp14<<<

Chapter 1

I swung my truck into a parking space at Hut's Burgers and then glanced at Logan in the passenger seat. He shot me a wide smile, his face half-hidden under the black Batman mask we'd picked up at Party City on the way here.

"You look fucking ridiculous," I said, dropping my gaze to his tattered jeans and long-sleeved "roadie" T-shirt. "That's not even a costume."

"Is too," Logan retorted, pulling down the visor to check his reflection. "I'm Batman."

Even under the stupid mask, I could tell he was waggling his brows.

"No," I pushed the door open to my truck and shot back, "you're a moron in a black mask."

Falling into step beside me as we crossed the parking lot, he tugged the sleeves down on his shirt to cover his signature tattoos.

"Look, its Halloween," he whined. "You told me we could stop and get some grub if I didn't draw attention to myself." Smiling, he motioned to his mask. "Done."

Pausing as we passed a group dressed like the entire cast from

Star Wars, Logan ogled the chick in the gold bikini with her hair wrapped in tight buns around her ears.

"Princess Leia." He nodded appreciatively. "You look hot. You want to visit the 'bat cave'?"

You want to visit the bat cave? *Seriously?*

If anyone else used a line like that, they'd get their ass handed to them. But not Logan. Even with half of his face covered, that cocky grin of his got the girl to stop in her tracks. Since I wasn't wearing a costume, and my face was nearly as recognizable, I stared down at my boots and didn't make eye contact with the chick.

Leia pulled out of her trance and shuffled closer to the guy in the Luke Skywalker costume. "I don't go out with bats." She sniffed. "Sorry."

From the way her eyes raked over Logan's lean frame, she *was* sorry. Sorry that her boyfriend was there.

"But you date your brother?" Logan retorted, shifting his amused gaze to the guy at her side. "You do know that Princess Leia and Luke are brother and sister?"

He laughed when the couple shifted uncomfortably at the revelation.

Tugging his sleeve, I grumbled, "Dude, let's go. I'm not going to debate fictitious genealogy with these two."

Shaking my head, I wandered toward the packed restaurant, hoping like hell Logan was behind me. With those long legs of his, he passed me a couple seconds later.

"Get the stick out of your ass, Wikipedia," he chided, holding the door open for me. "You're ruining my fun."

"This isn't smart." Following him inside, I gazed over all the crowded tables. "This place is balls to the walls."

"You should have worn a costume if you were worried about it."

I bumped into his back when he slowed to a snail's pace to gawk at a booth full of girls clad in tight tank tops and cut-offs. A smile tugged his lips as he admired a sexy brunette.

Twirling her hair around her finger, she cocked her head as she tried to place him. Her eyes drifted over his shoulder to the dirty window where the billboard for our band was clearly visible across the street.

When I saw the glint of recognition on the chicks face, I nudged him toward the counter.

"Keep walking," I hissed.

Reluctantly, he did as I asked.

"Relax, Wikipedia," he said, taking his place behind a line of patrons waiting to place their orders. "You look like you're chewing on a turd. Maybe that's why you don't get laid."

Ignoring him, I picked up a worn menu from the counter. "Yeah, that gets me in the mood to enjoy this mystery meat you insist on eating."

He rocked back on his heels. "You can look all day long." His grin widened. "None of those double-meat burgers are going to turn into a salad."

Hut's did, in fact, have salads. And at any other burger joint that's what I'd be ordering. But I wasn't going to pass up a golden opportunity to sink my teeth into a Big Bopper. Not that Logan needed to know that.

He narrowed his eyes while I pretended to weigh my options.

"Next!"

He swung his gaze to the impatient voice and then sauntered to the register.

Placing his order, he flirted shamelessly with the cute little waitress wearing Minnie Mouse ears.

She barely spared him a glance as she shoved the tray in his hand.

Logan looked at me feigning a shiver. "Brrr," he mouthed, giving the angry little mouse a once over before ambling away to stake out a table.

Chuckling, I took my place in front of Minnie. It was rare that women didn't notice Logan. He had a knack for attracting pretty girls, even before he was famous. And this girl was definitely pretty. Tousled blond hair fell in waves around her shoulders. And even though she was wearing a boxy Hut's T-shirt, I could see the outline of her magnificent rack hidden beneath the loose fitting, cotton fabric.

When she lifted her gaze, piercing green eyes fringed with heavy lashes bore into mine.

"What can I get you?" Her fingers hovered over the keys on the register, a scowl tugging the corners of her pouty lips.

"I'll take a Big Bopper with cheddar cheese. Make it a combo."

She sighed as she tapped in my order. "Fries or onion rings?"

"Neither." Giving her my most genuine smile, I reached for my wallet. "But could you make the bun gluten-free?"

Her skeptical green eyes wandered over my long hair and day old scruff. "That's a buck-fifty extra."

Judgmental much?

"Not a problem, Minnie." Chuckling, I zeroed in on the little triangle of black paint on the tip of her button nose. "I can afford it."

"Not saying you can't." She shrugged and handed me a paper cup. "But I'd be more worried about the heart attack on a plate than whether it was served gluten-free."

"Mel!" A woman shuffled out from behind the grill, wiping her hands on the fur of her grease-stained bunny costume. "What have I told you about your attitude? I don't care how tired you are, you don't take your bad mood out on the customers."

The bunny turned to me with a forced smile while Mel looked down at her toes.

"I'm Patty, the manager here. I apologize for Mel, she's a little . . ." Blinking, her gaze shifted to the picture of our band in a spot of honor on the Hut's "Wall of Fame." She swallowed hard, color rising in her cheeks. "Are you Christian Sears?"

"Nope." Smiling, I threw her a wink. "But I guess I nailed my Halloween costume."

Patty smirked, swinging her awestruck gaze to Logan, huddled in a booth a few yards away. "Tell Batman I'm a huge fan," she gushed, tossing some napkins and a straw on my tray. "I caught one of your shows at The Parish a couple months ago."

"We appreciate that. Glad you enjoyed yourself."

She brushed my arm aside as I tried to hand Mel my credit card.

"On the house." Patty cut her eyes to Mel, consternation furrowing her brow. "For your trouble."

Mel winced, snaring her bottom lip between her teeth.

"Its fine, really. Mel here was just giving me a hard time." I grinned at the cute little mouse, hoping she'd play along. She shot me a glower for my trouble.

"I insist," Patty said, shooing me away with a smile. "We'll have your food right out. Happy Halloween."

She whispered something into Mel's ear and then stalked away. Mel's green eyes met mine for a second before she followed her boss behind the industrial grill. My stomach sank when Patty shook a finger in Mel's face, her voice rising over the sizzle of the burgers and fries.

A bubbly redhead darted to the counter, her ponytail swinging behind her. "Is there something else I can get you?" She peeked at the customers impatiently rumbling in a line behind me.

Tearing my gaze from Mel, who was now defending herself, *loudly*, I shook my head. "Um, no thanks. I'm good."

After filling my drink at the soda fountain, I joined Logan at our table. I scowled at his grin as I slid into the booth. "What?"

"Don't get all pissy with me. I'm not the one who blew our cover." He popped a fry in his mouth. "I can't take you anywhere."

"Whatever."

Reclining against the cracked vinyl, I shifted my gaze to the open kitchen where Patty was glowering at Mel, the ears on her bunny suit flapping as she shook her head emphatically. Mel fumbled with the tie on her green apron before shrugging out of the smock and tossing it at her boss's chest. Her mouth moved in what I could only assume was a parting insult, because she turned on her heel and stormed off a second later.

Too enthralled with the drama, I didn't notice the redheaded waitress with the ponytail standing in front of our table.

"Here's your Big Bopper," she said cheerily, my burger resting on a plate in the crook of her arm.

I nodded, fishing a twenty out of my pocket to cover the tip.

"Hey, do you know what happened to the girl who took my order?" I asked casually, tossing the bill on the table. "The blonde?"

"Oh, that was Melody. I think Patty just gave her the heave-ho. That girl doesn't need to be working in the service industry anyway." Her ponytail swung back and forth as she shook her head. "She just called Patty a 'dragonian.' Call your boss a dragon, and you're asking for it."

I choked a little on my Dr. Pepper. "Do you mean 'draconian'?"

"Yeah." Her brows pulled together. "Isn't that what I said?"

I was about to correct her when she blinked at me without a hint of guile. I could be wrong, but she might be destined for a career in food service. And, hey, she seemed fine with that. Giving her a lesson on nineteenth century Greek was a waste of my breath and her time.

"Well, I guess it's a good thing she's gone." I stared into my cup. "She probably didn't fit in around here."

The redhead shrugged, clearing some trash off the table before grabbing her tip and scooting away.

Logan took the last bite of his burger, eyeing me as he chewed. "Dude, it wasn't your fault the chick got fired. She called her boss a dragon."

My appetite gone, I pushed the plate aside. "Draconian, you moron."

Logan crossed his arms over his chest. "And I suppose there's a difference, Wikipedia?"

I was about to suggest that Logan go ask the redhead for a date when I noted his expression. His eyes were lit with the same curiosity he'd tried to hide in high school when I'd offer to help with his homework. He'd act like he wasn't paying attention, doodling on his notepad with indifference. But I always smiled when he'd bust out with some obscure factoid, usually to silence a teacher who'd put him on the spot.

"Draconian means rigorous." I took another sip of my soda. "Severe and cruel."

Logan nodded slowly. "So it's kind of the same thing then, right?" Flashing a cocky grin, he snatched the pickle spear nestled next to my untouched burger. "Dragons are severe and cruel."

Chuckling, I picked up my Big Bopper. "You got me there, bro."

Chapter 2

The tension knots in my neck disappeared the minute I set foot inside the UT Life Science building. The ceilings in the alcove, inlayed with rich, dark wood, gleamed in the autumn sunlight filtering through the high windows as I walked toward the marble arch leading to the Life Science Library. Gold letters encased in black granite marked my destination.

Passing through the glass doors, my boots squeaked on the polished stone floors as I made my way to the physics section.

When I rounded the corner, I found Mrs. Thatcher replenishing the stacks with books she picked out of a gray bin.

She slid a thick text onto the shelf, then glanced at me and smiled. "Good afternoon, Christian. That book you wanted finally came in."

My ears perked up as I gave her an index card containing my current wish list. "Really?"

She tucked the card in her pocket and then pried a copy of *Was Einstein Right? Putting General Relativity to the Test*, from the cubby.

"Popular book." She handed me the text, then turned on her heel, calling over her shoulder, "I'll see if we have any of the others in the system."

"Thanks," I mumbled, running my finger over the worn cover.

I'd read this book many times, but never an edition this old. Cracking open the spine, hand written notes adorned the margins, some dating back years from the looks of it.

Exiting the stacks, I headed toward the rows of uncomfortable wooden chairs. I wasn't complaining, though. Given the amount of time I spent in libraries growing up, it wasn't a good day unless one of my legs was numb or my back was screaming for mercy.

Settling into my usual spot at a table in the back, I reached for my phone to bring up my secret playlist of classical music.

My father, the mathematician, insisted rock and roll wasn't conducive to concentration. It was one of the few things we agreed on. Though I never let him know it.

As I slipped in my earbuds, I noticed a girl two tables away juggling an armful of books and supplies. Losing the battle, the texts slipped from her grasp, crashing to the concrete floor.

"Shit," she muttered.

Dropping to her knees, she tucked a swath of blond hair behind her ear before crawling under the table to retrieve a couple of wayward pencils.

One glimpse of her on all fours, her luscious ass in the air, and I jumped out of my seat.

The scent of cinnamon and autumn leaves assaulted me as I knelt to help her collect the papers littering the floor.

"Here you go," I said, handing over the messy pile.

Wobbling to her feet, she smiled down at me, her blond hair curtaining her face. "Thanks. I'm all thumbs today."

Spying a cherry lip balm wedged against the chair leg, I plucked the tube from its hiding place and then rose to my feet.

"Cherry, huh?" The smile froze on my lips when I caught sight of her unusual jade green eyes. Silver lined the pupils, luminous under the fluorescent lights.

Trying to place her, I started at her blond hair, working my way down.

Pausing the descent when I reached her perfect tits, my gaze darted to hers. "Mel, right?"

Her plump lips fell into a frown as she snatched the lip balm from my hand.

"Melody," she bit out. "My friends call me Mel. And we're not friends, Christian."

Opening the flap on her backpack, she dropped the little tube into the abyss.

So, the angry little mouse remembered me. And she knew my name.

"Patty was right. You do have an attitude problem." I leaned forward, smirking. "How's that working out for you?"

"Patty's an idiot. And my attitude's fine. I just don't suffer fools." She tipped her chin, her gaze roaming over my face like I was the fool she was being forced to suffer. "Gladly, at least."

Unsure if I was turned on or insulted, I crossed my arms over my chest and studied her posture. *Insulted.* Definitely insulted.

"Saint Paul called—he wants his line back," I said blandly. "Didn't think I'd catch that, did you? Second Corinthians—chapter eleven, verse nineteen. Look it up if you don't believe me. And the whole 'not suffering fools' thing? I guess you're in the wrong business." Her frown intensified, which satisfied me immensely so I added a cherry on top. "Or you were, until you got yourself fired."

As I doubled back to my seat, I heard Mel's mint green Chucks squeaking against the floor as she stalked after me.

"I did not get myself fired," she hissed, dropping her backpack on the table with a thud. "You were there. I made one comment." She held up a finger. "*One.* And bam . . . I'm out the door."

"Calling your boss 'draconian' probably didn't help." I leaned back in my seat, smiling at the fire in her eyes. "Although the general consensus at Hut's is that you called her a dragon."

She blinked, stunned into silence.

"A dragon?" she finally croaked, her shoulders quaking with wry laughter as she looked down. "Well, that figures."

All that jiggling drew my gaze straight to her breasts. Even if Melody was a haughty brat, she was a haughty brat with nice tits.

Scowl firmly in place, I adjusted myself before she looked up. But I needn't have bothered. One look at that cold gaze and my balls shriveled.

"Well, like I said, I don't deal well with stupid," she chirped, slinging her backpack over her shoulder. "So, if you'll excuse me."

She smiled a totally fake, sweeter than sweet smile, then trotted away toward the stacks.

I stared after her, watching her hips sway.

Fuck me, the girl was rude. And hot. Hot, rude, and obviously smart, since she disappeared into the dusty heap of books that made up the biochemistry section of the library.

Too unnerved to concentrate on Einstein's theory of relativity, I ripped a hand through my hair. That damn girl ruined my book buzz. And called me stupid.

Slamming my text shut, I pushed to my feet and then took off for the archives.

I found Mel sitting cross-legged on the floor amid a pile of books and notes.

She looked up at me and rolled her eyes. "What do you want?"

I was about to reply when I caught a view of her tantalizing cleavage. *Those*, I thought to myself.

For some reason—probably because I'd yet to tear my gaze from the firm, round globes beneath her blouse—the sixteenth letter of the Greek alphabet jumped into my head. Pi—the ratio of the circumference of a circle to its diameter.

Before I embarrassed myself reciting the most rudimentary mathematical constant known to man, I thrust the book on Einstein's theory at her.

"I'm reading a book on the theory of relativity, I'll have you know."

My less than witty retort earned me a smile. And a mocking one at that.

Dropping back on her palms, Mel primly crossed her legs at the ankle, appraising me.

"So, I'm assuming you're here because you got stumped on one of the big words?" She arched a perfect brow. "I'm a little busy. But the librarian has a science dictionary." Pointing in the direction of Mrs. Thatcher's desk, she added, "It's the big book with words you can't pronounce. Just point and grunt—she'll probably get the picture."

"You're a presumptuous little thing, aren't you?" She didn't answer so I crouched to examine her pile of books. "What's all this for, anyway?"

"Busy here," she muttered, her eyes darting from her textbook to the notepad on her knee.

Ignoring her subtle—scratch that—*blatant*, attempt to get rid of me, I smiled when I came across a copy of *Genetic Manipulation of the Nervous System*.

Close enough.

I tapped her leg with the corner of the book. When she lifted her annoyed gaze, I looked deeply into her green irises.

Before I got lost in the depths, or that damn sweet scent of hers, I said, "Did you know that only two percent of the population has green eyes?"

Thoroughly unimpressed, her lip quirked. "Good to know. If you're done regaling me with generic information—"

"Generic? I don't think so." Placing the heavy text back on the pile, I continued, "The field of study is still evolving. It's only recently come to light that there are about fifteen genes responsible for determining eye color."

That fake ass smile tilted her lips once again. "You wouldn't happen to be able to name any of those pesky genes, would you?"

Mel wrinkled her nose in the most adorable way as she issued the challenge. Which was going to make stomping her ass all that much more satisfying.

The first rule of thumb when you're about to pose an argument: never ask a question if you're unsure of the answer. Guess they didn't teach her that in chem class.

I blew out a breath as if contemplating. But the only thing I really wondered was what color steam would come out of her ears when I was finished.

"Well," I drawled. "I don't have time to name them all, but the OCA2 and the HER2 are the most common. The appearance of blue, green, or hazel eyes results from the Tyndall scattering of light in the stroma." Her lips parted, and I gave her a mock frown. "You do know what the stroma is, right? That *pesky* fibro vascular layer of tissue behind—" Shaking my head, I sighed. "Never mind, it's too complicated to explain right now. Let's start with something simpler—like brown eyes. That's pretty easy. The shade of brown in the eyes is directly related to the melanin in the—"

Jumping to her feet, Mel glared down at me. Her gaze followed mine as I stood. Since I had almost a foot on the girl, she was now glaring *up* at me, but the stone cold expression never changed.

"I know what the determinates of brown eyes are, thank you very much," she spluttered through clenched teeth.

"Sure you do." Lowering my tone, I winked. "Don't worry. I won't tell any of your buddies that I stumped you with an explanation of the iris pigment epithelium."

If Mel's lack of verbal skills was any indication, she was even more enraged. Good. One last dig and my work here would be done.

Enunciating slowly, I leaned in to make my point. "The epithelium is in the *back* of the iris, in case you were wondering." I glanced over the books and notes at our feet. "You've obviously got some studying to do, so I'll let you get back to it."

I knew damn well she probably could recite everything I told her in her sleep. The fact that she assumed I didn't know any of it is what bothered me.

I took a step back, my smile dissolving when her hand shot out to fist my T-shirt. For a second I thought she might hit me. Instead, she rose to the balls of her feet.

The last thing I saw before her mouth crashed into mine was the fire flashing in her jade green eyes. And then there was nothing but the sweet taste of her lips, and the cinnamon and autumn scent that surrounded her.

Deepening the kiss, Mel slid her tongue over mine, stroking gently.

If this was her way of winning an argument, I was all for it.

Nudging her against the bookcase, one hand disappeared in her hair. And the other? It was everywhere.

My name in the distance forced my attention to the end of the aisle. I blinked at Mrs. Thatcher, frozen in her spot with her palm molded to her hip. Her gaze fell slowly to my wandering hand that had somehow found a home on Mel's ass.

"Allow me to repeat myself since you didn't hear me calling your name, Christian," the librarian said brusquely. "I got that book you wanted on the Fender bass."

Mrs. Thatcher then turned a speculative eye on the girl still trapped in my arms.

"Melody, you know better than this," she admonished. "I have no problem verifying your research hours for Professor Riser, but if you're planning on researching your own anatomy, you need to do it on your own time."

Stepping in front of the little spitfire to keep her from getting us kicked out, I said, "We were just—"

"I know what y'all were doing," Mrs. Thatcher interjected. "You just can't do it here."

Gripping my bicep, Mel stepped around me.

"I-I'm sorry, Mrs. Thatcher," she said, employing a soft tone I didn't think she possessed. "I was just . . . my boyfriend came by to see me and . . ." Stammering, her cheeks brightened to the color of ripe tomatoes. "We were just . . . leaving."

Falling to her knees, Mel hastily gathered her things. She shoved a book in my hand, which I accepted without question, then crammed the rest of her notes into her backpack.

Curling my hand around her arm when she finished, I helped her to her feet.

Mel swallowed hard, shifting nervously as she addressed Mrs. Thatcher with a tight smile. "If you wouldn't mind not mentioning this to Professor Riser, I'd really appreciate it."

A smile ghosted the librarian's lips as she folded her arms over her chest. "That'll cost you an hour of reading to the kids in the daycare center to make up your time. Deal?"

"Deal." Melody's shoulders sank in what I assume was relief. "Thank you, Mrs. Thatcher."

Stiff as a statue, Mel didn't look at me until the librarian's footfalls were out of earshot.

"Give me my book," she growled.

I chuckled at her attempt at a fierce glare. "Boyfriend, huh?"

"Obviously, that was for Mrs. Thatcher's benefit. I already lost one job; I can't afford to have my professor questioning my research hours."

I tucked her text under my arm. "Are you researching genetics?"

Shifting her fiery gaze to the book I was holding for ransom, she pondered her response for a long moment. My smile more or less assured she wouldn't get what she wanted until she answered my question.

She closed the distance between us, her hot breath tickling the hollow of my neck. I thought she might kiss me again—which I was totally down for—so I relaxed.

Big mistake.

Her greedy fingers shot out and snatched the text before I could react. Studying me with an unreadable expression, she held the book like a shield to ward off my advances. Which was funny as hell since *she* was the one who kissed me.

Composing herself, she took a step back and then sighed. "At the moment I'm concentrating on proteins." She offered a curt smile, all business. "I'm a Beckman Scholar, so if you'll excuse me, I've got a lot of studying to do."

Swooping her backpack from the floor before she had the chance, I nearly fell over from the weight of the damn thing.

"There's really no excuse for you, sweetheart," I deadpanned.

Sweetheart? I wasn't sure if she had a heart—sweet or otherwise. But she damn sure tasted sweet. Cherry lip balm lingered on my lips from the searing kiss, the memory of her velvet tongue sending a tingle to the base of my spine.

Seizing the moment, and her blessed silence, I slid my hand into hers. "You're rude, arrogant, and presumptuous, just like I said. But you're also kind of cute. So I guess I'll let you buy me a cup of coffee and tell me all about your research."

Chapter 3

$\mathcal{W}$ aiving the fondue fork over the vegetables in the tiny bowls, I smirked at Mel. "Keep 'em closed."

We'd been playing this game since we arrived at the Melting Pot, the fondue joint we finally agreed on for dinner.

Agreed being the operative word. I'm sure it was easier negotiating the Treaty of Versailles. And once we'd arrived, prying any personal information out of Mel was a battle unto itself. So I issued a challenge: if she guessed the right blend of cheese and the vegetable or meat, I'd answer any question she posed. And vice versa.

Mel took a sip of her iced tea, rolling her eyes. "Try not to burn me this time, okay?"

"Didn't your mama ever teach you to blow on something hot before you put it in your mouth?"

Her gaze turned wistful and she shook her head. "Must've missed that lesson."

I paused, my foot finding hers under the table. I'd known the girl for less than a minute, but I could tell that the comment hit a nerve. Why I cared, I didn't know.

Breaking the awkward silence, her lids fluttered closed. "Do your best," she said with a sigh.

Watching Mel while I skewered a piece of broccoli, I dipped it in the Alpine cheese mix. She looked so fucking cute with her mouth open and that pink little tongue sticking out.

"Okay . . . try this." I blew the steam off the morsel before lifting the fork to her lips.

A smile curved her mouth at the gesture. "You didn't have to do that. I can blow myself."

All the blood rushed from my head and the utensil slipped from my grasp, splattering cheese everywhere.

"Shit. Mel . . . I'm sorry."

Grabbing my napkin, I reached across the table. My hand landed on her breast as I tried to clean the goopy mess.

Her eyes widened, either from my groping or the stain spreading across her blouse.

"Give me that." Snatching the checkered cloth, she glared at me. "What are you, sixteen? Get your mind out of the gutter. I'm a woman. I can't possibly blow myself."

Mel was crazy if she thought that's where my mind went. It was her pouty lips wrapped around my dick that had me squirming in my seat.

What the hell? I wasn't *that* guy. Maybe Logan was rubbing off on me.

Banishing the thought, I averted my gaze while Mel cleaned up. When I turned back, spotting the outline of her nipple peeking through the fabric where the oily glob had been, my mouth went dry.

Kill me now.

"You're the one with your mind in the gutter," I lied, my eyes glued to her face. "The fork slipped."

I almost forgot about our little game until she picked up the chunk of broccoli. She examined the tidbit thoroughly before popping it into her mouth.

"Broccoli and Alpine." She smiled as she chewed. "I win."

The chick was competitive in a way that usually turned me off. But anything that came out of that smartass mouth had the opposite effect.

Lacing my fingers behind my head, I reclined in the booth. "Fine. Ask away." I smiled coyly. "Anything goes."

Pondering, her eyes drifted to the window in the front of the restaurant where my brand new Ford F250 truck sat parked next to her old Jeep.

"What's it like to get everything you ever dreamed of?"

Locked in her gaze, I brushed my thumb over a spot of cheese clinging to her cheek.

"What makes you think I get everything I want?" Unable to pull away, my hand lingered on her smooth skin. "Nobody gets everything they want, angel."

I realized I'd been had when her lips quirked.

"So you're not going to answer?" Her smile turned triumphant. "Cool, I win again. Close your eyes—my turn."

Contemplating her next choice, her fork hovered over the half-empty melting pot.

"There's no way to answer that question," I groused, but did as she asked. "So, you didn't really win."

Humming to herself, she slipped a piece of food between my lips.

"Shit!" I spit the wad in my napkin. "What the fuck was that?"

The picture of innocence, Mel blinked at me. "If you can't guess, then technically . . . "

"I lose, right?" I grabbed her legs under the table and she yelped. "That was dark chocolate and cheddar cheese on sourdough." I swallowed hard at the aftertaste. "So, I didn't lose...and this question is going to be a doozy."

Leaning back, she kept her knees between my legs. "Shoot."

"What kind of protein are you studying and why?"

Mel's smile fell away. "That's two questions."

"Okay . . . what kind of protein are you studying?"

When the waiter appeared at our table to fill our glasses, Mel sealed her lips tight, her knees bobbing steadily.

Watching his retreating back, she said quietly, "Right now I'm concentrating on Tau protein."

Keeping up on the latest medical technology was a secret passion of mine, but the name was unfamiliar. "Tau?"

Nodding, she reached for her glass of iced tea. Her eyes widened as she took a swallow. Searching the room, she zeroed in on our waiter.

Confused, I squeezed her leg. "Mel, what is it?"

Ignoring my question, she called the kid over. He scurried to the table, his mouth falling into a frown at Mel's scornful expression.

"Is this sweet tea?" she demanded, tension lines etching the corners of her mouth.

"I believe so," the server stammered. "I—"

"Take it," she snapped. "I ordered unsweetened." Softening her tone at his stunned expression, she handed him the glass. "Please . . . if you wouldn't mind."

I waited until the kid scrambled for the kitchen to say, "Easy there, guns. It's just a little sugar."

Her brows drew together. "Sugar kills."

"Don't you think you're overreacting just a bit?"

She lifted a shoulder and stared into her lap. "Maybe," she said softly.

Mumbling an apology when the waiter returned, Mel didn't look up until he left.

"Sorry about that," she said to me sheepishly. "Free question—anything you want to know."

I raised a brow. "Anything?"

Nodding, her lip disappeared between her teeth as my hand slid higher on her leg.

"Eggs or pancakes?"

She cocked her head. "You mean . . . in general?"

"I mean specifically." Tracing circles on her jean-clad thigh with my thumb, I smiled. "I'd really like to know what you want me to make you for breakfast in the morning."

Chapter 4

*P*inning Mel to the cinder block wall in her tiny living room, I kissed her deeply, my fingers creeping under the hem of her blouse. She sighed, the back of her head bumping against the concrete as I palmed her breast.

"Fuck . . . sorry." My hand disappeared into her blond locks, searching for a lump. "Are you all right?"

The girl had me so revved up I was ready to take her right here, inches from her front door.

Resting her hand on my chest, she laughed softly. "No permanent damage. I've got a hard head."

Mel was hardheaded, all right. And smart. Not to mention sexy as hell.

She slipped out of my arms, heading for the kitchen before I could devour her mouth again. I bit my lip when she ducked her head into the fridge, wiggling her ass as she poked around.

"Would you like something to drink? I've got water and . . ." She walked back with two bottles of Dasani. "Water."

"Water's fine."

Twisting the cap off the bottle, I looked around the tiny apartment. Mel's place was as bare bones as it got. Campus housing with concrete walls and worn carpet. Her entire kitchen would fit nicely in the guest bathroom at my house.

Sinking onto the arm of the recliner, Mel snagged her lip between her teeth.

"I've never had a one-nighter," she admitted, her usual confidence wavering. "So you're going to have to tell me how this goes."

Gazing around the room, I noted the large calendar on the dining room wall, a neat stack of books on the table below. Farther to the right sat an assortment of colored highlighters, lined up precisely like soldiers waiting to be recruited.

The girl was organized—OCD style—which was refreshing. But the fact that she was already planning for my imminent departure unnerved me.

Closing the gap between us, I twirled a lock of her hair around my finger.

"It goes the way it goes, angel. The only thing set in stone is your breakfast. Eggs, right?"

She looked up, the sparkle in her eyes faint at best. "I'm not expecting you to be here in the morning, Christian. We both know what this is. I've heard all the rumors. I'm not naïve, you know?"

I pulled away out of sheer reflex. All night long we were just Christian and Mel. My celebrity was barely mentioned. Hell, she didn't even pump me for information about the band.

After a moment, I eased onto the chair.

"Really?" Sliding an arm around her waist, I tugged her onto my lap. "What have you heard about me? I'm dying to know."

Staring at the bottle in her hand, her fingernail skated over the label. "The usual. Oversexed rocker. Never in one place more than a night. That kind of stuff."

Tucking a finger under her chin, I tilted her face to mine.

"I've been in Austin for months, so you shouldn't believe everything you hear."

Her dull expression indicated she saw through my halfhearted attempt to address the rumors. I may have been in the same city, but that didn't mean I was in the same bed. A Google search would turn up dozens of pictures to prove the point.

Mel nuzzled closer, fighting to keep her smile. "I'm just letting you know that I get it. Guys like you don't date—they fuck." Her brows drew together. "And breakfast isn't usually part of the deal."

Tightening my grip, my thumb skimmed the smooth skin above the waistband of her jeans. Conversations like this were usually unnecessary. The chicks I hung out with knew the score. Hell, they were fine with it. No truths exchanged beyond the basics: hotel or tour bus, and where should the cab drop you off when we're finished.

But Mel wasn't like that. She spent her time in libraries, not waiting behind rope lines hoping to get my attention.

Taking her hand, I blew out an apprehensive breath and then began, "I've been on the road for four years. It's a little hard to plan breakfast when you don't know what city you'll be in come morning. But I can't blame it all on my lifestyle."

My stomach knotted at the admission. It felt strange to say it out loud. Maybe I was more like my bandmates than I cared to admit.

Prying my tongue from the roof of my mouth, I went on, "From a strictly biological standpoint, you know, attraction fades as soon as the hormone rush is over. Pheromones and all that."

Chancing a peek at Mel's face, I found her nodding in agreement, her green eyes glued to my face. If anyone understood chemicals it was the beautiful little geek on my lap.

I traced a finger over the curve of her jaw, smiling. "I'm not saying I'm opposed to a repeat performance. I just don't believe in making promises I can't keep."

Mel's gaze slid from mine as she mulled over my declaration. Despite the passionate kiss at the door, she wasn't a sure thing. Mel could ask me to leave. Hell, she might.

The realization hit me in the chest like a five hundred pound boulder as she shoved to her feet.

Hand on her hip, she studied me for a long moment.

"But you will be making *me* breakfast . . . is that what I'm hearing?"

Not quite a question, but a statement of fact. There would be no pre-dawn walks of shame with this girl.

"You can bet on it, angel."

Surprised at how quickly the answer flew from my lips, I pushed off the chair.

Intent on capturing Mel's mouth, I was surprised when she linked our fingers and said breezily, "Cool. Now that we got that out of the way, I think I'll take you to bed."

She was taking *me* to bed.

Maybe I should have invited her to my place and shown her who was really in charge.

I scoffed at the thought as Mel led me through the dark apartment. Taking girls to my place was on the top of my "never do" list. The one and only time I had, the crazy chick showed up the following day with an overnight bag.

My solid "no" on the subject turned to a definite "maybe" in the ten feet it took to reach Mel's room.

Releasing my hand, she scampered around, gathering clothes from the floor and the bed.

"Sorry," she said as she dumped the pile on the chair in front of her desk. "I didn't expect any company. "

Her statement thrilled me, though I wasn't sure why. Mel didn't seem to share in my delight. Slumping on the corner of the mattress, a pink flush stained her cheeks as she looked around at the mess. Obviously the control she exercised in the rest of her life didn't extend to her bedroom.

Attempting to lighten the mood, I fingered the mouse ears peeking out from under some papers on her nightstand. The same mouse ears she wore the day we met.

"Maid's day off?" I joked.

She let out a staggered breath.

"I am the maid." Her eyes widened and then she quickly amended, "Not here, of course. But it's one of the many glamorous jobs I've held in the past few years."

"A maid, huh?" Nudging her onto her back, my mouth dropped to her ear as I fished the button of her jeans through the hole. "Please tell me you've got some little see-through uniform around here and a pink feather duster."

Molding her palms to my shoulders, her thumb glided back and forth over my collarbone. "I think they'd frown on that at the nursing home."

Nursing home . . .

A burger joint and a nursing home. The only job I ever had before we started the band was helping my dad with his lesson plans when I was in high school.

Sliding next to her, I propped up on my elbow, appraising her profile. "Tough gig, huh—working your way through school?"

"Not really." She lifted a shoulder. "All this is paid for through my scholarship. I'm actually really lucky."

Sadness dimmed the sparkle in her eyes when she swung her gaze to mine, belying her assertion.

I brushed my thumb over her bottom lip, removing it from the prison of her teeth. "So, you don't have to work?"

"The scholarship doesn't cover everything." Her eyes darted away again. "I have other expenses."

Glimpsing this softer side of Mel made me want her that much more. I wanted to be inside her. To feel every part of her. But I didn't want to push.

Caressing her stomach, I kept my hand in the "PG" zone as I pressed a kiss to the side of her mouth. Mel responded by reaching for my belt. Her brows drew together when I caught her wrist.

Smiling, I lifted her hand to my lips and kissed her knuckles.

"You first, sweetheart."

Burying my face in the crook of her neck as I unzipped her pants, I breathed in her autumn scent. As I hooked my fingers into the sides of her jeans, a random thought popped into my head.

Rising to my knees to slide the denim over her hips, I asked, "When do you graduate?"

A smile broke like dawn, lighting her whole face.

"December fifth." She beamed. "Best Christmas present I could ever ask for."

Out of nowhere, a twinge of regret echoed in my chest. "That's awesome, Mel. Really."

Lost in thought, I shoved to my feet and began to undress. I felt her eyes on me as I unlaced my boots, so I cut my gaze to hers.

"What is it?" Defensiveness crept into my tone.

The girl had me off balance, like maybe she'd decide I wasn't her type. I chuckled inwardly at the thought, because I wasn't her type.

Mel rolled onto her side. Propping on her elbow, she rested her chin on her upturned palm. "Did you ever think about going to college?"

Dragging my T-shirt over my head, the twinge of regret in my chest grew more insistent. I'd spent one semester at UT, out of respect for my father. But there was no way I was getting into that with Mel.

Clutching the foil packet I'd retrieved from my wallet, I eased her onto her back, using my body weight to press her into the mattress.

"How do you know I didn't go to college?" I fiddled with a lock of her hair. "Is it that obvious?"

I refused to look away, even though I knew the answer would be in her eyes, regardless of what she said.

"No. I just thought . . . with your career, I assumed—"

"You assumed right." I brushed a feather light kiss to her nose. "I had to choose between school and music."

"You chose right." A smile curved her mouth as she ran her thumb over my bottom lip. "You're a brilliant musician. And you can always go back to school."

Unable to hide my surprise, I rose with my palms planted on either side of her face.

"You like Caged?" I lifted a skeptical brow when she nodded. "I don't believe it. Name one song. And not that damn ballad that crossed over to the pop charts."

Rolling her eyes, she sighed in mock irritation. "'Devour.' Third cut, second CD." She raised a brow of her own. "Happy now?"

"Ecstatic."

For whatever reason it was important to me, knowing that Mel appreciated my music. I realized I was staring down at her with a goofy smile when she laid her palm against the tattoo of the lion's head on my chest.

"This is the cover art from the first CD, right?"

When I nodded, Mel pressed her lips to the ink. My fingers slid into her silky hair, holding her against me for a fraction of a second longer than I should.

Dropping back onto the pillows, Mel traced her fingertips over the intricate design, frowning. "I wish my tattoo was this cool."

Me of all people should know better than to judge a book by its cover. Still, a little teasing seemed to be in order.

"You have a tattoo?" She nodded but I didn't let up. "I call bullshit. You're going to have to show me."

She nudged me off, and I slid down beside her.

Whipping the blouse over her head, she turned on her side. Gathering her hair on top of her head to expose her neck, she looked over her shoulder and said, "It's—"

"Euler's Identity." I traced the set of numbers with my index finger.

Flipping around to face me, genuine surprise coated her features. "Impressive. Most people think it's just a bunch of numbers."

Euler's Identity, in all its complexity, could never be described as a "bunch of numbers." Anymore than Shakespeare's sonnets could be likened to "a bunch of words." Euler's Identity was mathematical beauty.

Spoken like the son of a mathematician.

A dark cloud threatened in the distance as I thought of my father. Rather than wallow under the weight of his disappointment, I unfastened Mel's bra and then coaxed her onto her back so I could feast on her rose tinted nipples.

"The tattoo is perfect. Like these." Laving one pebbled tip, I rolled the other between my thumb and forefinger.

She arched, and I gladly complied, sucking the stiff peak into my mouth. Slipping my hand inside her panties, my fingers crept toward her heat. She was soaked. Ready for me.

Parting her slick folds, I brushed my thumb against her clit. "You like that?"

"Yes." She squirmed. "More."

The girl with all the answers was suddenly reduced to one-word responses. Smiling smugly, I inched down her body, tasting all the smooth skin on my way. She beat me to my destination, her fingers buried in the lace by the time I reached the apex of her thighs.

"I'll take care of you, angel." I caught her wrist and then ran my tongue along her fingertips, savoring her spicy sweetness. "I promise. I got you."

She looked down at me over the swell of her breasts. "I don't think . . . I mean . . . you can try."

Biting her lip, she turned her face into the pillow, her brows drawn together.

"Try?" I tugged her panties over her hips and discarded them on the floor beside her jeans. "I'll do more than try."

"I think there's something wrong with me," she admitted, a weak smile tilting her lips. "I've never been able to . . . you know . . . come that way."

Settling between her legs, my eyes never left hers as I slipped a finger inside her slick core. Stroking her deeply, I found her G-spot. "You mean this way?"

She gripped the comforter, her lids falling to half-mast. Within seconds her hand snaked down to rub her swollen clit. "Yes . . . no . . . I mean . . . I can do it."

But I didn't want her to do it. I wanted to do it for her. Normally, I wouldn't care. Hell, normally, I didn't have to care.

"Trust me, baby." I dragged her hand to her side. "You're going to come."

I stroked her tiny nub while she strained against my grip.

"More...oh, God," she moaned. "I want to come. Please . . ."

"Patience, angel." I worked her a little harder—a little faster. "Does that feel good?"

"Yes, but—"

"How about this?" Adding another finger, I traced her clit with the tip of my tongue.

"Yes . . . yes . . ."

She wiggled her hand, desperate to break free and aid me in my efforts.

"Please, Christian . . . I can't . . ."

Releasing my hold, I kept her away by entwining our fingers.

Frowning in dismay, her nails dug into my skin. "I don't think . . . it won't work . . ."

I kept up the pace until she grew silent, the tension ebbing from her body.

Burying her free hand in my hair, she guided the rhythm.

There you go, angel. Show me how you like it.

With every flick of my tongue and twist of my hand, I brought her closer. And then she shattered, a string of incoherent phrases tumbling from her lips as she clenched around me.

Licking and stroking, I didn't stop until she cried out again, riding the wave of another orgasm. She tasted so fucking good, I could've stayed there all night, but my dick was on the verge of a full on revolt.

Working my way up her limp body, I nibbled each of her nipples along the way.

When I finally reached her face, her lids fluttered open.

"There she is." I pressed a kiss to her mouth. "You still with me?"

"I think so." She panted. "That's never . . . I haven't . . ." Her skin flushed the most adorable shade of pink. "I've always had to do it myself."

My rock hard cock begged for relief at the visual. Tearing open the foil packet with my teeth, I slid the condom into place. Every muscle in my body tightened as I lowered myself on top of her. My tip at her entrance, her wet heat beckoned, so I slid in an inch.

"I wouldn't mind you showing me that sometime." Thrusting all the way in, I rocked against her until she relaxed. "But we're going to try it my way first."

Chapter 5

"Christian . . ."

The soft moan dragged me from my sleep. After two rounds of the most unforgettable sex of my life, Mel's groans had probably etched their way into my gray matter. Smiling, I rolled over, ready for round three. Patting the empty space, moisture dampened my palm.

Sitting bolt upright when I heard another moan, I looked around the dark room.

"Mel? Where are you?"

"Christian . . ." she choked. "Help . . ."

Heart racing, I stumbled to my feet, nearly tripping over the body crumpled next to the bed.

"Melody?" My hands slid against her clammy, sweat-soaked skin as I cupped her neck. "What is it?" Alarmed by her blank expression, I barked, "Tell me!"

Knocked from her haze, she blinked.

"J-juice," she stammered through chattering teeth. "I n-need juice."

Gazing at the perspiration soaking her heavy cotton T-shirt, I swallowed the panic rising in the back of my throat.

"Hold on."

Racing to the kitchen, I pulled open the fridge and then grabbed the full bottle of Tropicana. Aiming the spout into the cup I found on the counter, juice splattered everywhere.

Get your shit together.

Taking a deep breath to steady myself, I finally managed to fill the cup. My false confidence drifted away when I rounded the corner of the bedroom and found Mel huddled against the nightstand, her eyes hooded and her arms limp at her sides.

Crouching, I pressed the mug to her lips. "Drink this, angel."

Pushing my hand away, sticky orange liquid spilled down the front of her shirt.

"No," she mumbled, "l-leave me a-alone. I don't want a shot."

She continued to babble, too far gone to realize what she was saying.

Gripping the back of her hair loosely, I tilted her face to mine. "Mel, listen to me. You've got to drink the juice."

At the sound of my voice, her unfocused gaze locked on mine.

"There she is," I said as I lifted the cup to her lips. "Just a couple of swallows, okay?"

Curling her fingers around mine, she grasped the cup and fought to take a few sips. Her body rejected the plan and she coughed, spilling a good bit on her lap.

"It's okay. It's just a little juice." I sifted my digits through her matted hair. "Are you a diabetic?"

Confusion glazed her pretty green eyes as she nodded her head.

After cajoling her to take another drink, I eased her back against the nightstand.

"Where's your test kit?"

Shaking her head, Mel rasped, "More juice."

I thought about asking her again, but chances were until the fog cleared she'd fight me. So I nodded, angling the edge of the cup to her lips.

Shaking her head, one small fist held me off as she took the glass with a shaky hand.

"I'm okay," she mumbled after taking a few tiny sips. "In fifteen minutes . . . I'm okay."

Fifteen minutes?

I calculated the number of things that could go wrong in fifteen minutes. Nine hundred seconds. A lifetime.

Lowering my head to examine her face, I found no comfort in her dazed expression.

"Mel, let me take you to the—"

"Fifteen m-minutes," she repeated, her green eyes pleading. "Please."

Dropping on my ass, I pulled her onto my lap, and to my surprise, she let me. I pressed my fingers to her wrist, calculating the beats as I held her.

Fifty-three. Not bad, but not good.

I wedged a knuckle under her chin and then tilted her face to mine. She let me do that too, but she didn't seem happy about it if her creased brow was any indication.

"Angel, your pulse is a little sluggish. Maybe I should call the doctor."

The silver threads surrounding her pupils sparked as the fire returned to her gaze. "No. I'm f-fine."

As the minutes ticked by, Mel's breathing steadied. Releasing her death grip on my arm, she left half-moon indents from her finger-nails on my skin.

"Sorry," she mumbled, attempting to scoot off my lap.

"Why don't you tell me where that test kit is?" I held her in place. "You need to test your sugar."

Placing a kiss to her temple, I rocked her gently until she finally relented, her shoulders sagging in defeat.

"Black pouch—bathroom drawer," she whispered.

I pushed to my feet and then slid my arms under her legs to lift her.

Glaring, she flattened her palm against my chest. "I've got it."

Ignoring her defiance, I scooped her up and placed her on the bed. A small smile curved my lips when she scowled.

Yeah, she was definitely better.

"Stay put." I raised a brow. "I mean it. Don't make me tie you to the bed."

Jutting her bottom lip out, Mel crossed her arms over her chest as I turned to walk away. I glanced over my shoulder in time to find her creeping toward the edge of the bed. Doubling back, I glared down at her.

She lifted her gaze in surprise, one foot poised to hit the ground,

"I wasn't joking about tying you up," I rumbled.

Reluctantly, she retracted her leg.

"Good girl." Pressing a kiss to her forehead, I warned, "Don't move."

Darting into the bathroom, I flipped the switch on the wall, flooding the small space with light. I rooted around in the only drawer, finding the black pouch hidden in the back, like it was a deep, dark secret.

Checking my reflection in the mirror, my hand reflexively went to my side, my fingers digging into the taut flesh covering my ribs. I'd broken two of the damn things almost a year ago, but no evidence remained of the injury.

Diabetic. At twenty-five.

Daily shots. A restricted diet.

I cringed when I pictured her face at the restaurant.

"It's just a little sugar."

The words rang in my ears as my gaze shifted to the orange streak of juice on my chest.

Guilt ridden, I turned off the light.

Entering Mel's bedroom, I held the black pouch like I had the winning lottery ticket. "Got it!"

My cheery tone evaporated when I spied the empty bed.

Stalking to the dresser, my jaw torqued so tight I thought it would snap, I bit out, "Are you hard of hearing, or is English not your first language? I told you to stay put."

Clutching a fresh T-shirt, she glowered at me. "I'm all wet. I need a shower."

Taking her elbow, I guided her to the bed while she did her best to shake off my grip.

"After you test your blood sugar."

She snatched the kit from my hand and then dumped the contents on the mattress. "My sugar's fine. I know my body."

"Not well enough, apparently."

I received a cold stare for my trouble. But I didn't care.

Rubbing the back of my neck, I winced at the pop from the little pen she held to her finger. Instinct kicked in at the sight of the crimson droplet that bubbled from her skin, and I stepped back.

"Squeamish?" She squeezed the blood onto the test strip and then met my gaze, tilting her chin defiantly. "You don't have to stay. I got this."

Chewing the inside of my lip to keep from biting her head off, I turned my attention to the monitor on the small handheld machine.

"All good," Mel announced when the device beeped.

Gathering the supplies, she shoved them back into the bag.

I caught her by the wrist. "Are you normal?"

"Of course I'm normal," she snapped, her eyes hard enough to bend steel. "I'm just a diabetic."

"I meant, is your sugar normal?" My thumb traced small circles on her palm. "Just tell me, Melody."

She dropped on the side of the bed, looking down at her toes. "It's still a little low."

Easing beside her, I laid a tentative hand on her thigh. "What happened?"

"I forgot to take my shot. And, I, um . . ." Her brows drew together. "I was in a hurry, and I mixed up my dosage."

"How—"

"Because I wasn't paying attention, all right? I was sleepy." Swaying when she stood, she placed a balled fist on her hip. "Sorry you had to see it. I'm going to take a shower. You can let yourself out."

Snaking an arm around her hips before she could get away, I pulled her onto my knee.

"Are you kicking me out?" I rested my chin on her shoulder. "That's just cold, angel. It's the middle of the night."

There was no way I was going to leave her here alone after her little episode. Even if I had to humble myself in the process.

"Stay if you want." She pushed to her feet. "I'm taking a shower."

Weaving as she made her way across the room, she stopped to brace her hand on the doorjamb and take a few deep breaths.

Stubborn.

My chest bumped her back as I followed her to the bathroom.

"I'm fine," she insisted.

"I'm sure you are." Nibbling her neck, the faint taste of salt lingered on her skin. "I just want to see you naked."

I felt her quiver, but it wasn't desire. She was still weak. I maneuvered her against the wall in the bathroom despite her meek protests. Pulling the stained T-shirt over her head, I admonished myself to stay on task when I glimpsed her erect nipples. Apparently, my cock wasn't as sympathetic to Mel's plight as the rest of me. One peek at those rose tinted beauties and he was raring to go.

"My shower's the size of a coffin," she said, her gaze falling to the tent in my boxers. "So no funny business."

"Got it. No funny business."

I looked down at my dick and then up to her face, shrugging when he didn't obey.

A chuckle tumbled from Mel's lips as she turned on the water. "Don't say I didn't warn you."

My cock jumped at the sight of her, bent over in only her white cotton panties. I cursed under my breath, annoyed. The fact that I was ready to set the recent harrowing experience aside and bend the little spitfire over the counter unnerved me. I wasn't some horny teenager. I got more ass than your average guy by double. Hell, triple.

Mel slipped off her panties and then ducked into the shower, where I joined her a few minutes later when my dick finally decided to cooperate.

To say the stall was like a coffin gave coffins a bad name. I prayed I didn't have to spend the afterlife in someplace this cramped.

Biting back a groan when Mel's ass grazed my crotch, I grabbed her hips to keep her from doing it again.

"Are you trying to kill me?" I nipped her shoulder. "There's only so much I can take. And given the circumstances, you're not making this any easier."

"Circumstances?" She spun around—difficult to do in the enclosed space—but she managed. "There are no circumstances. I told you I was fine. If you're just here to babysit me, you can take your ass—"

Cupping the back of her neck, I crushed my mouth to hers. I couldn't think of anything else to do to shut her up. That acid tongue of hers tasted a hell of a lot better tangled against mine.

She responded by deepening the kiss. Fighting to gain purchase against my slick body, her legs shook from the effort.

Before I lost all reason, I sank my teeth into her bottom lip. Her eyes flew open and she glared at me. I was getting used to the glare, so I went about my business, squeezing a dollop of shampoo into my hand.

She groaned as I slid my fingers into her hair.

"Feel good?"

Instead of answering, she wiggled closer. I guess she planned on wearing me down.

Massaging her scalp, I brushed a quick kiss to the corner of her mouth. "Later. And you better quit pouting, or I'm going to bite that lip again."

"But..."

Nudging her head under the streaming water, I drowned her protest. She fused her eyes shut to avoid the deluge of soap, her brow furrowed in consternation.

As my fingers traveled the length of her tangled locks to expel the suds, I examined every freckle on her upturned nose. Following the water sluicing down her body, I zeroed in on the small bruise on her stomach where she'd administered the insulin injection.

Her fingers splayed over the area, knocking me out of my trance.

"There's nothing wrong with me," she insisted, blinking against the water trickling into her eyes. "It's a condition, not a disease. I can do anything anybody else can do."

The angry bruise on her unmarred skin told a different story. A painful story.

"I'm sure you can." Allowing myself one taste of her sweet mouth, I smiled against her lips. "And in a little while, I'm going to let you prove it."

Chapter 6

*M*y head pounded as I surveyed the dance floor from our perch in the VIP area at Maggie Mae's. Sipping my lukewarm beer, the bitter aftertaste matched my sullen mood.

"I haven't seen you in a week and you've barely touched your first beer," Logan groused, sliding a fresh bottle in front of me. "What the fuck is up with you?"

"I'm driving."

Logan paused with a shot glass halfway to his lips. "Don't give me that shit. You're the most responsible asshat I know." Nodding to my phone resting on my knee, he quipped, "I bet you've got Yellow Cab on speed dial. What's really going on?"

Another sip of piss warm beer. "I don't know, dude. Cinnamon withdrawal."

"Huh?" Concern lit Logan's blue eyes. "Is that serious?"

Apparently, it was dead fucking serious.

"I made it up. Just a joke—see?" I pointed a finger at my forced smile. "There's nothing going on."

I suspected my cinnamon remark was spot on, but I wasn't about to admit it. This was the first night that I hadn't spent with Mel. The only night since we hooked up at the library seven days ago.

After leaving Mel's place that first morning, I had no intention of calling her for a few days—at the very least.

But somehow my truck ended up in the parking lot of the Life Science building after band practice that afternoon, like the damn thing had a mind of its own.

I told myself that I was only there to check on Mel because I was concerned—like any friend would be.

Apparently I was so fucking concerned, I broke my cardinal rule and invited her to stay the night at my house. Actually, I lured her there under the guise of mind-blowing sex. And then I fucked her into oblivion, and she fell asleep in my arms.

We repeated the ritual the next day. And the next.

She'd even pulled me over to join her study group. Twice. I guess it was easier than explaining the guy lurking in the stacks, stealing glances from afar.

We never made any formal plans though, I just showed up after practice, and it was her place or mine.

Until tonight.

I mentioned the show to Mel this morning while I had her up against the wall in her coffin of a shower, even hinting that she should drop by The Parish.

Who was I kidding? I practically gave the girl a fourteen-carat-gold-plated fucking invitation. I thought she'd jump at the chance. Or at least hop. People lined up for hours to see us perform.

But not Mel. She told me she had a morning class and staying out late didn't jive with her schedule.

Since she made it clear that she wasn't going to change her plans, there was no reason for me to change mine. The band always went out after a show. But I hadn't counted on being pissed and cranky. And Logan's inquisition wasn't helping matters.

He continued to appraise me with narrowed eyes, examining the beer in my hand like I had a fever or something.

"Are you going to tell me what the deal is or just sit there and sulk?" Logan elbowed me in the ribs to tear my attention from my phone.

I had Mel's number pulled up, ready to send her a text.

"Nothing's going on." Pocketing the device, I pushed aside the old beer in favor of the fresh bottle. "I guess I'm just not in the mood to party."

Logan abandoned his interrogation mid sentence, turning his attention to a group of scantily clad women teetering up the steps leading to the VIP area. The bouncer held open the velvet rope, and the girls sauntered in.

Logan reclined against the cushions, grinning wide. "Well, you better get in the mood, bro. 'Cause we got company."

The loud music camouflaged my discontented groan when Sean, our drummer, strode into the VIP area, balancing an overfilled tray of shots on his upturned hand.

"Y'all look like you're in desperate need of company." Sean slid the drinks on the table and then threw his arm around the redhead glued to his side. "I met Brandy here backstage after the show." His lip quirked as his hand drifted to the girl's ass. "I convinced her and her friends to come hang out with us for a while."

From the coy grins on their faces, the girls didn't need much convincing.

Looking around for the nearest exit, my gaze landed on a blond in a short skirt. Her long, toned legs were the stuff dreams were made of. But apparently not mine, since my dick barely twitched.

I continued to stare at her, wondering what those long legs would feel like wrapped around my waist.

Still nothing.

Fuck, I really *was* tired. Tipping my head back, I polished off the last of my beer, keenly aware of the phone in my pocket. It was still early. Kind of. Maybe I could call Melody and . . .

"You're Christian, right?"

I blinked up at Blondie who'd somehow managed to slink across the room without me noticing.

"That I am."

"I'm Allison." She pressed her leg against my knee. "You guys were awesome tonight."

Cutting her gaze to Logan, chatting up a brunette on his right, Allison's face fell for a millisecond.

Logan was the big-ticket item, while I was merely a consolation prize. It never bothered me before, but right now the look of disappointment clouding Allison's baby blue's when she gazed at me sent a rush of anger straight to my frontal lobe.

This chick didn't want me. She wanted to fuck me. Or Sean. Or Cameron, if he was here. That being said, she'd dump any of us like a stone if Logan batted an eyelash at her.

"That's always nice to hear," I said, barely able to contain my boredom with the whole conversation.

Taking a sip from the fresh beer I'd commandeered from the table, I shifted my gaze to Allison's breasts out of habit. The large mounds spilled from her low-cut blouse, firm and juicy. And I could tell by the way those puppies didn't budge when she laughed, they were fake as hell.

I glanced down at my palm, which fit very nicely around Mel's small, soft breasts. And her ass. Her thigh . . .

Logan nudged my shoulder, offering me two shots from the tray.

"Where are your manners, son?" He gave Allison a wolfish grin. "Aren't you going to offer this pretty thing a drink?"

Allison giggled loudly, her eyes sparkling in the dim light. I was relatively sure she'd take on both of us if we asked.

Not that I was judging. Sex was sex. Pheromones, hormones, and attraction. Girls weren't immune, and condemning them for their desires wasn't my style. If they wanted to have fun, I was all about it. Usually.

Hesitating for a moment, the thought of Mel lingered in my brain. Seven nights was six more than I'd ever spent with any woman. And that was probably the reason I felt so shitty. Too much of a good thing. Mel was just one appetizer on the buffet.

I gazed around at the other girls vying for attention, wondering if any of them were as tasty. If any of them smelled like cinnamon and fresh leaves and . . .

Shaking my head to knock Mel's image from my mind, I took the shot and made room for Allison on the couch.

"What do you say, Allison?" I patted the cushion and she nestled in beside me, her hand on my thigh. Ignoring her cloying perfume when my lips touched her ear, I pressed the drink in her hand. "You in the mood for a shot?"

My heavy lids creaked open as the taxi pulled to a stop. I paid the fare before stumbling onto the curb, my eyes wandering to the second floor. With an unsteady gait, I stumbled toward the concrete staircase. In my condition, I probably shouldn't be attempting such a feat. But I did.

Holding tight to the railing, I navigated the steps. When I reached the landing, I staggered to the door, the ground tilting beneath me.

Blowing out a breath, I rapped three times in quick succession.

What the fuck are you doing?

The errant thought drifted right out of my head when I met Mel's sleepy green eyes.

"Christian?" Her brows drew together in confusion. "What are you—"

Pulling her into my arms, my uncoordinated hand slid to the curve of her ass. "Did you miss me, angel?"

I wasn't crossing the threshold until she gave me some kind of clue. It's bad enough that I'd shown up here out of the blue. That I sent Allison packing because the thought of her lips on mine was so revolting, I couldn't even kiss her, let alone take her up on whatever else she was offering.

"You're drunk," Mel said, resting her palm on my shoulder to steady me. "What are you doing here?"

"Answer my question first."

Bracing my hand against the doorframe, I did my best impression of a sober person while she scrutinized me with a small frown.

"You want an answer?" She crossed her arms over her chest. "Go home."

"That wasn't the question."

Was it?

Hanging my head, I attempted to recall what I'd asked. Inebriated as I was, time had no meaning, so I wasn't sure how long I stood on Mel's stoop, staring at my shoes.

Apparently, long enough for her to take pity on me.

"Get in here." Mel's fingers twisted in the fabric of my T-shirt before she pulled me inside. "I'm freezing my ass off and I need to get some rest."

Though I tried to resist—or maybe just thought about it briefly— I let her drag me all the way to the bedroom.

"Don't you dare throw up on me," she mumbled, sliding between the sheets.

"Wouldn't dream of it."

As I snuggled beside her, befuddled and totally at peace, my heavy lids closed.

"To answer your earlier question: *yes*."

Her soft voice pierced the thin veil of near sleep as she traced a finger back and forth across my forearm.

"'Yes' what, angel?" I murmured, savoring the scent of her autumn-soaked skin.

"Yes, I missed you."

I draped my denim-clad thigh over her leg so I could pull her closer. And though every cell in my body came to life, I was too wasted to do anything about it. The funny part? I didn't care.

"You're not an appetizer," I murmured, sneaking a hand under her nightshirt to caress her bare stomach.

"Good to hear," she said through a yawn. "But the next time you show up on my doorstep in the middle of the night, you'd better bring a blanket, because I won't let you inside."

Burying my face in her hair, the evening's tensions fell away.

"Yes you will."

If she argued the point, it was lost on me. I was already out. Floating on a cloud of cinnamon and surrounded by fall leaves.

Chapter 7

*W*histling to myself, I pulled into the parking lot of the Life Science building.

Over a week had passed since the night I showed up drunk on Mel's doorstep. I'd woken up completely dressed with a pounding headache. Mel didn't help matters, reading me the riot act in a tone just below a screech.

But the little experience at Maggie Mae's proved one thing: I was burnt out. I needed to chill on the partying and recharge my batteries. And since I enjoyed spending time with Mel, there was no reason I shouldn't take advantage of this little lull.

I'd be back to myself in a couple of weeks. Max. But in the meantime, I could enjoy the awesome sex and great company.

An autumn fling.

Since the girl smelled like a fall day, it seemed appropriate.

Jumping out of my truck, I double-timed it toward the building, checking the clock on my phone. *Shit.* I was late.

Tonight was Mel's research study group, something I looked forward to despite the chilly reception I'd received from her buddies the first time I showed up.

My celebrity meant nothing to the science geeks that made up her team. If anything, it was a strike against me. But after the second session, when I'd solved a complex math problem that nobody else could figure out, the group realized I might have something to offer beyond leering at their fearless leader. I wasn't a member of the team by any means, but at least they stopped treating me like a pariah.

Slowing to a jog when I entered the library, my lips curved into a smile when I spotted Mel at a corner table, surrounded by her ardent followers. She was a rock star in her own right, she just had a different kind of stage on which to perform.

Mel arched a brow as I strolled up, pointedly looking over her shoulder at the large clock on the wall.

"Sorry," I mouthed, giving her a wink as I flopped onto the empty chair next to hers.

Our plans were fluid, so no apology was necessary. But Melody rewarded the gesture with a soft smile and a warm hand on my thigh.

Totally worth it.

Her cohorts nodded at me, some even offering smiles.

Only one guy still seemed irritated by my presence: Mitchell, the graduate student with the big mouth and the bigger ego.

Slinging his arm over the back of his chair, Mitch's mouth twisted in something between dislike and flat out hatred. "Christian, nice of you to join us. We were just discussing human beta cells. I don't suppose you've got anything interesting to share."

From the way Mitchell looked at Mel, she was the only thing he wanted me to share. And there was zero chance of that happening. Not that she'd be interested in Mr. Crewcut.

Mel's acid tongue got the better of her before I could reply. "This isn't Quiz Bowl, Mitchell. Christian doesn't—"

Brushing my foot against Mel's under the table to silence her, I pulled a stack of papers from my backpack.

"Well, I'm not an expert like you, Mitch, because—you know—I have a life," I quipped. "But I did find this article on some diabetes research they're conducting at Mt. Sinai using stem cells." I slid the copy across the table. "Take a gander. I'm sure Melody would be happy to explain anything you don't understand." Covering her hand with mine, I beamed at her with pride. "Wouldn't you, angel?"

A few chuckles erupted from the group, mostly hidden behind textbooks or coffee mugs. Mitchell might be a big deal for all I knew. But in this group, Mel was the leader. And she proved it every time she opened that pretty little mouth. The same pretty little mouth I planned on plundering as soon as I got her alone.

Mitch the Bitch dismissed the article with barely a glance. "This is old news. Its good to know you can use Google, though. That's always handy."

Opening my mouth to level the dude, I stopped cold when Mel's fingers inched toward my crotch.

"Let's take ten everyone," she announced, pushing out of her seat. "It's been a long night."

Whatever she had in mind was probably better than punching out the geek in front of me, so I gave Mitchell a smug smile and then shoved to my feet to follow my girl.

My girl?

Dismissing the thought as some kind of caveman reaction to Mitch's presence, I slid my arm around Mel's waist as we passed Mrs. Thatcher's desk.

"Where are we going?" I whispered.

Pulling me into the hallway, she looked around like she was casing the joint.

"This way," she whispered.

Stepping around a yellow cone marked Out of Service in front of the ladies room, a triumphant smile curved her lips when the knob twisted in her hand.

"Melody, do you know what 'out of service' means?" I paused in the doorway. "I don't even want to know what's in here."

Walking backward, she fingered the top button on her blouse. "You sure about that, rock star?"

So, she wanted to play? Even if I had to don a HAZMAT suit, I wasn't turning that down.

"You threatening me with a good time?" I flipped the lock on the door and then stalked toward her. "That's not wise."

Spinning her to face the large mirror in front of the row of sinks, I pressed my chest against her back. She groaned, pushing back against the sizable bulge straining my zipper.

Nibbling the skin at the crook of her neck, I worked the button on her jeans and then slipped my hand inside her panties.

"Fuck, you're wet." Sliding a finger inside her slick channel, I ground my erection into her backside. "Looks like I got here in the nick of time. What have you been studying, angel?"

She mumbled an incoherent reply, her hand following mine into her panties.

"No you don't," I growled, nipping her ear. "You need to learn to keep your hands to yourself."

"That's what I'm trying to do." Exasperated, she fought for control, wiggling her ass to distract me. "We've only got a few minutes."

In the short time we'd been seeing each other, I'd discovered a dozen ways to give the girl an orgasm. But I usually spent half my time trying to keep her from finishing the job herself.

"I'd love to play around with you, but since we're in a hurry," I slid her jeans and panties to her knees, "we're going to try something new."

Eyes narrowed, Mel tracked my movement in the mirror as I slipped the silk scarf off her neck. "New?"

"Hands behind your back."

My request was somewhere between a growl and a plea.

Gaze locked on mine, she worried her bottom lip. "Why?"

She knew the answer. I could see it in her eyes. But I didn't want to scare her off the plan. To Mel, control was almost a religion.

Adopting a playful posture, I rocked my hips, grinding harder against her bare ass. "Why not?" I sucked her earlobe between my lips, my eyes never leaving her reflection. "Tick-tock. It's up to you."

Slowly, Mel placed her hands behind her back.

"That's my girl."

My dick throbbed as I loosely bound her wrists.

"Christian . . ." Tugging at the restraints, her eyes widened. "I don't know . . ."

Locking our gazes in the mirror, my palms sculpted the rigid planes of her shoulders.

"I've got you, angel. I promise." I pressed a kiss to her neck. "Trust me."

Slipping my fingers inside her hot, wet folds, I found her swollen nub. The worry lines creasing the corners of her mouth faded as my index finger glided over her clit.

"You like that?"

Her eyes fluttered closed as I thrust two fingers deep inside her pussy. "Yes. Oh God . . ."

Reaching under her shirt, I freed one breast from her flimsy bra. Her head fell back against my chest as she rode my hand, straining to find her rhythm as I pinched her nipple.

"Feel good?"

Need edged the hue of her jade green eyes, along with the ever present worry.

"Don't . . . don't . . . stop . . . please . . . I want . . ."

Anxiety, her worst enemy at times like this, also became mine. The sooner she let go, gave in to the pleasure I offered, the better.

"Relax, angel." My thumb began a relentless assault on her clit, applying the gentle, even pressure she craved.

"Feel that?" I growled, pressing my cock against her bound hands.

Curling her fingers around my denim-clad shaft, she nodded.

"That's for you. All for you."

My words sent her over the edge. Arching her back as she came, she bit her lip to keep from crying out. Her muscles clenched around me, dragging me to the brink as wave after wave crashed over her.

"That's it, baby." Scoring my teeth along her neck, I continued to massage her G-spot until I was sure she was finished.

Her trembling legs nearly gave out when I pulled away.

Frantically, I searched my wallet for a condom.

"I need to get inside you," I rasped. "Like, right now."

Shoving my jeans to the floor, I tore the foil packet with my teeth.

Mel twisted at the restraints, but she said nothing as I rolled the latex into place.

"Easy, baby." I placed a gentle kiss on her shoulder. "Lean over for me."

She did as I asked, tipping forward.

Raking over her body with a feral gaze, a single word tumbled around my head: *Mine.*

My palm slid from her silky hair to her bound wrists as the notion wrapped around my brain: *Mine.*

"Christian . . . ?"

Knocked out of my stupor, I cleared my throat.

"I'm right here." Fisting my shaft, I ran the tip of my cock along her slit. "Tell me you want me, angel." The evidence of her arousal was all over me, but the voice in my head demanded an answer. When she mewled an incoherent reply, I slid inside an inch. "Tell me, Melody."

"I want you . . . I want . . . "

Burying myself in one thrust, I growled, "This?"

"Yes . . . yes . . . harder . . . *please* . . . "

Grasping her hips, I slammed home with enough force to rattle the sink.

I paused, fully seated, admonishing myself for the lack of control.

"Shit. I'm sorry. Did I hurt you?"

"No . . . no . . . I'm good . . ." Sincerity suffused her tone. "Keep going . . . do it again."

My fingers delved inside her slick heat, circling her clit with languid strokes. A strangled moan tumbled from her lips, rewarding me for my efforts.

Grasping Mel's shoulder with my free hand, I continued to thrum the tiny bundle of nerves as I pounded into her.

Determined to take her with me, I bit out, "Come for me, angel. Let me feel you."

The soft moans she fought to stifle broke free. She called my name, her walls closing tight around me.

Mine.

Two more thrusts and I stilled, erupting inside her. The aftermath of her orgasm pulled at me as I ground out the last bit of sweet release.

"Fuck, baby . . ." I pressed my forehead to her shoulder blade as I tugged the knot on the sash to untie her. "That was . . ."

The all-time best sex I've ever had. And that's saying something.

Uncharacteristically silent, Mel cut her gaze to mine out of the corner of her eyes as she dressed, her lips bent in a frown. Maybe she wasn't as down for this little game as I was, but she seemed to be enjoying it at the time.

Taking her hand, I ran my thumb over the indent on her wrist. "If you wanted me to untie you, all you had to do was say so."

She smiled, albeit warily. "It's not that."

I tucked a fallen strand of hair behind her ear. "What is it then?"

She blinked up at me, concern etching her features. "You don't want me to touch you?"

"What gave you that idea?"

She cocked a brow, glancing at the crumpled scarf draped over the sink.

Pulling her to me, I brushed a kiss to her pouting lips.

"I'm not worried about you touching me." Capturing her hand, I brought it to my cheek to prove the point. "I'm worried about *you* touching *you*. That's my job. I'll always take care of you."

She pondered, her lips set in a thin line like she didn't believe me —or, as I feared, she wasn't on board with the whole restraint thing in general.

I rubbed my neck, my expression neutral. "We don't have to do it again. I just thought you might like it."

It wasn't the first time I'd gone outside the box, played a little game to amp up the tension during sex. With Mel, the extra stimulation was totally unnecessary. The girl had my number in the bedroom. Or the bathroom. Really, any room that she was in—naked —and I was done for. But she was always so impatient, like I might leave her hanging. I thought she might enjoy a little extra spice.

A blush crept into her cheeks as she turned to the mirror to check her makeup. "It was kind of hot. And very ingenious."

A bit unsettled, I buried my nose in her hair and breathed her in. "Seriously Mel, I'm not going to lie, that was—" *unforgettable,* "really good, but we don't have to do it again if you don't want."

Spinning around, she rose to her tiptoes and pecked my lips. "Don't put words in my mouth. I wouldn't mind trying that again sometime."

A ringing endorsement, in Mel speak. Which more or less guaranteed we'd be doing it again. And again.

As she led me toward the library, I had to wonder: *who was really in charge?*

An image of Mel bent over the sink popped in my head. *Her.* She was definitely in command. But as long as she took me along for the ride, I was good with that.

Mel's steps faltered as we entered the library. "I think we were gone longer than ten minutes," she mumbled, picking up the pace.

My hand fell to her ass as we walked. "You should be thanking me then. It would have been much longer if—"

"Shut up." Her lips twitched as she stared straight ahead, a deep flush creeping from her collar when I gave her a squeeze.

"Just sayin'." I pulled her chair out. "Could have been worse."

Ignoring my chuckle, Mel plopped into her seat and grabbed her diet soda. The smile ghosting her lips turned to a frown as she gazed around the table at her team. Mouths open, they gaped at her. I got the feeling when Mel said fifteen minutes she was usually waiting with a stopwatch.

"What are y'all looking at?" she snapped. "Get back to work."

When I gave her foot a gentle tap, she softened, shrinking against the wooden chair. A couple of her friends let out audible sighs.

Crisis averted.

While I thought "scary" Mel was hot as hell and only slightly intimidating, her study buddies didn't share the feeling. Except one. Mitch the Bitch.

Tapping his pen against the table, Mitchell cleared his throat. "We were about to pack it in." He tipped his chair back on two legs. "But now that you've decided to grace us with your presence, maybe we can continue."

Leveling a withering glare on her cocky research partner, Mel snarled, "I was taking a break, Mitchell. But if you've got something better to do, by all means, *go*."

Ignoring her little dig, Mitchell's chair hit the floor with a thud as he appraised her. The irritation was still there, along with something else. Concern?

"You look a little flushed," he noted. "Is everything okay?"

Squirming, Mel's gaze met mine before shifting back to Mitchell's. "'Course." She shrugged. "Why wouldn't it be?"

Shaking his head, Mitchell scowled. "Mostly because you just said 'course' instead of 'of course.'" Throwing his pen on the table, he ran an agitated hand through his cropped hair. "Maybe your brain's a little foggy. Have you checked your sugar lately?"

Only my quick thinking kept Mel's butt in her seat. When she started to rise, my hand clamped down on her thigh. To my surprise, she didn't fight my hold.

"I'm fine," she hissed. "My health is none of your concern."

Eyes blazing, he leaned forward. "That's where you're wrong. In case you forgot, this whole damn project centers around diabetes research. The management of your disease is of great concern to the group."

"*Condition*," Mel snarled. "It's a condition."

"No, it's not." Plucking a book from the reference pile, Mitchell flung the text across the table. "Look it up. Diabetes is a disease. And your lifestyle changes of late are taking a toll." His gaze swung to the other members of the team, before settling on Mel. "Everyone can see it."

A chair scraped the concrete floor as Brent, one of the undergraduates, pushed to his feet.

"It's been a long night and I'm not up for another debate on this subject," he said wearily. "I'm out of here." Hoisting his backpack over his shoulder, he lifted his chin to me. "Nice to see you again, Christian. Night y'all."

Mel watched as the rest of the group gathered their things, making similar excuses. She jolted when Mitchell slammed his book shut.

"See what I mean?" He shoved his files and textbooks into his backpack. "People are starting to question your commitment. You're not yourself. You've got a real shot at being published. You'd better think long and hard before you throw it all away," his hard gaze shifted to me, "over *nothing*."

Since I was the "nothing" the bastard was referring to, I slowly rose from my chair. I towered over the little prick by at least four inches, but Mitchell didn't back down. Impressive, but it wouldn't keep me from pounding his ass into the hardwood floor.

"Listen, dude," I growled. "You don't know—"

Mel gripped my arm tightly. "Sit down, Christian." She looked up at me, eyes beseeching. "You don't understand."

Fists clenched at my sides, I dropped back in my seat, leveling my fiercest glower at Mitchell. Anywhere else and the dude would be eating pavement. But I had respect for the library. And even more respect for Mel.

"Keep it civil, dude," I warned. "You don't want to mix it up with me. *Believe me.*"

The little twerp turned his attention to Mel. They locked gazes in a silent power struggle and to my utter amazement, Mel blinked first.

"I'm not throwing anything away, Mitch," she said with a little more conciliation than I was comfortable with. "You're making a big deal out of nothing. We've got less than a month left until graduation. I've worked my ass off for years. My studies have always come first."

Mitchell honed in on her hand, still resting on my bicep.

"There's still work to be done, *Melody*. You're the one that's interested in pursuing other research at UT. The extra credit stuff will go a long way toward getting the grant for—"

"Don't worry about my future, Mitch." The old Mel was back, irritation lacing her tone. "Worry about your own."

He gripped his travel mug so tight his knuckles lost color. "Fine. I'll do that."

Frowning, she watched his retreating back as he stalked away.

I resisted the urge to follow Mitchell and pummel him into the pavement for speaking to Mel like that. The two obviously had history, shared goals that I knew nothing about. I wouldn't fuck that up by beating the douchebag senseless. Though I really, *really* wanted to.

"That guy needs a lesson in manners," I remarked as I helped Mel collect her notes. "He's lucky I didn't kick his ass."

She crammed the papers into her backpack before hoisting the strap over her shoulder.

"Drop it, Christian." A weary sigh fell from her lips. "I've known Mitchell for a long time. He's a valuable member of my team. Let's just leave it at that."

Irritated, I slipped the heavy pack off her arm. "Your place or mine?"

Yanking her sweatshirt from the back of the chair, she wrapped her arms around her middle and then took a step back.

"Neither," she said quietly, looking down at her toes. "I've got a lot of work to do, so I think we should call it a night."

Chapter 8

Fumbling with the strings on my bass, I winced as the sour note bounced off the walls in our rehearsal space. Logan slammed his microphone into the stand, then turned a murderous glare in my direction.

"What the fuck is up with you, Christian?" Gripping his blond hair in frustration, he paced in a circle. "It's a simple fucking chord change."

"Give it a rest, Logan," Cameron said with a sigh as he lifted the guitar strap over his head.

Feedback screeched from the amp, drowning out Logan's retort as Cameron stalked to the row of stands to stow his instrument.

"You owe me one," he said, bumping my shoulder on his way to the mismatched couches in the corner.

Cameron's phone was out and he was already tapping the screen before his ass hit the cushions so I doubt whether his motives were completely pure.

Sean climbed down from his drum kit and stretched his legs. "Thank fuck," he grunted, eyeing Logan on his way to the fridge. "What's with the three hour practices, anyway?"

Logan's piercing blue eyes burned with barely contained agitation as he watched Sean take a seat next to Cameron. When he cut his gaze to me, I saw something more.

Guilt.

Six months ago, Logan personally kicked our manager to the curb while we were in Dallas playing a rock festival. Lindsey Barger, the bitch the record label handpicked for us was a lot of things. Stupid wasn't one of them.

Before we'd even returned to Austin, Lindsey was back in Los Angeles, waging a private war against the band. Labeling us "divas" and "hard to handle," she continued to badmouth us at every turn. As a result, our label was dragging their feet on renewing our contract. And without a contract there was no new material to promote, so we were stuck. Right back on Sixth Street, playing at The Parish where we started.

Things weren't critical—*yet*—we had two singles hanging by their fingernails on the Billboard 200.

But if we didn't set something up soon . . .

Some of the angst retreated from Logan's posture as he flopped onto a chair next to the one I'd staked out across from the couch.

"Y'all know I'm trying to set up an audition with Twin Souls, but they're not returning my calls," Logan admitted as he twisted the cap off his bottle of Shiner Bock. "I want to be ready when they do. That means we got to stay tight." He swung his gaze to mine and I shrank in my seat. "*Focused.*"

"You haven't heard anything yet," I said through a sigh.

Logan's blue eyes shot daggers straight at my forehead. "You think if the biggest management company in the business gave me a jingle I'd keep that shit under wraps?" He turned to stare into the distance, nodding to himself. "They'll call," he insisted, lifting the bottle to his lips to take a large gulp of beer. "It's only a matter of time."

I wanted to find the will to care, but right now I was too fucking irritated. And it had nothing to do with the band, which annoyed me even more. Here we were, talking about major shit that impacted my future, all of our futures, and I was losing sleep because I hadn't seen Mel in two days.

After our dustup with Mitchell at the library, she'd backed off on our nightly encounters. She told me she needed to buckle down and study, so I left her alone.

Fishing my phone from my pocket, I threw caution to the wind and then tapped out a text to Mel.

You know what they say about all work and no play? Hit me back when you're ready to play.

I shook my head, deleting the message. Cheesy wasn't the way to go.

Gazing at the blank screen for a long moment, I finally punched in: *Miss you, angel.* Finishing off the text with a smiley face emoji, which I never used, I pressed send.

When Cameron chuckled low in his gut, I discreetly set my phone aside.

"What's so funny?" I asked.

Cameron drained his beer and then pointed the neck of the bottle in my direction.

"You are." He chuckled again, with more gusto. "I know that look, man. Who is she?"

Folding my arms over my chest, I went for casual. "There is no *"she."* Just because you were bitten by the bug doesn't mean we're all going to catch it."

"You'd be lucky to catch what I've got." Cameron socked me in the arm on his way to grab another beer.

He was totally serious—whipped like a dog, and proud of it. He didn't even bat an eyelash when Logan and Sean started in, needling him about his newfound domesticity.

Cameron was never the player Logan was, but he was a close second. He left a string of broken hearts in every city we visited, until he met Lily Tennison during our ill-fated concert stop in Dallas.

Ignoring Tweedle-Dumb and Tweedle-Dumber, I twisted in my chair to meet Cameron's Zen-like gaze. "All of a sudden you've got it all figured out, huh?" I snorted. "You meet a chick and three days later you're a changed man—is that how it goes?"

"It was four days, but it don't matter." Cameron shrugged, reclaiming his seat. "When you know, you know."

"It's only been a few months," I responded, unable to keep the skepticism from my tone. "Let's see how Lily handles it the first time you have to pick up and leave for a year."

Cameron's hazel eyes turned cold enough to chill the air between us. "Lily's here to stay. She ain't with me because of all this shit." He motioned to the small stage and all our abandoned equipment. "It doesn't matter whether I'm home or in fucking Brazil, she ain't going nowhere."

I didn't want to burst his bubble, so I barked out a laugh. "I hope you're right. Since Lily's got your balls in her pocket, it would be awfully inconvenient if she disappeared."

A confident smile eased onto Cameron's lips. "Not going to happen."

I frowned at the unanswered text and let out a resigned sigh. "Well, Mel's not Lily."

I jerked my gaze to Logan's when a laugh erupted from his chest.

"So you're batting for the other team now?" he chided. "When did you start dating dudes? Does Mel have a cute sister you can set me up with?"

"I've seen some of the chicks that stumble out of your bunk on the tour bus," I replied blandly. "Maybe you should think about expanding your dating pool."

Choking on his beer, Logan's eyes bugged out.

"I love all women, Wikipedia," he said through a cough. "Don't judge. Especially since you're dating a dude."

"Not that it's any of your business, but I'm not dating a dude." Seizing my phone from the arm of the chair, I pulled up a picture of Mel and then shook it at Logan. "Does this look like a dude to you?"

Logan's smirk faded as he peered at the screen. "No, that's definitely not a dude."

Grabbing the device before I could stop him, Logan tapped the screen to enlarge the image.

"What the fuck are you looking at?" I snarled. "Give me the

damn phone!"

Batting my hand away, a smile tilted his lips. I knew that look; he was checking out her tits.

"Chill, man." After one more appreciative glance at Mel's photo, Logan tossed the phone at me. "I was just looking for the scar on her head."

I narrowed my eyes at the asshat's stupid grin. "She doesn't have any scars on her head, you moron."

Shrugging, Logan propped his feet on the table, his smirk firmly in place. "A chick like that's got to have some kind of defect if she's hanging out with you."

As I stared at the photo on the screen, the picture morphed into an image of Mel on the floor of her bedroom, shaking in a pool of sweat.

"Melody's not defective," I said quietly. "She's fucking brilliant, and she's perfect."

Silence blanketed the room. The awkward kind. Logan no longer smiled, but surveyed me with a blank expression that matched Cameron and Sean's.

"So, when do we get to meet this perfect woman?" Cameron asked, snapping the tension filling the air.

I was about to answer when my phone lit up with a text from Mel.

Miss you too. Come over after practice if you can.

The knot in my stomach unwound as I tapped out my reply.

On my way.

Jumping to my feet, I scooped my backpack from the floor. "Gotta jet. See y'all later."

Much later, I hoped. I owed Mel at least four orgasms, and I wasn't planning on letting her out of bed until I settled the debt.

"You didn't answer Cam's question," Logan called as I headed to the door. "When do we get to meet your imaginary girlfriend?"

Girlfriend?

I didn't have time to argue the semantics.

"Soon."

Chapter 9

My boots barely skimmed the concrete as I raced up the stairs to Mel's apartment. Since I didn't want Mel to know I was racing, I slowed my pace when I reached the landing. All my joy evaporated on the spot when she didn't answer the door.

Gripping the knob, the brass handle turned in my hand. What the hell—an unlocked door in this neighborhood?

"Mel?" My stomach fell as I entered the dark, silent living room. "Melody."

No response.

Adrenaline surged as I chewed up the worn carpeting in four or five strides. As I stormed into the bedroom, I met Mel's sweet smile. Propped against a heap of fluffy pillows, the skin on her bare shoulders picked up the glow from the candles strategically placed throughout the room.

"I'm right here," she said, letting the sheet fall to expose her breasts. "But I couldn't answer the door because I'm . . . you know . . . *naked*."

Overcome by the scent of autumn leaves and cinnamon, my wobbly legs carried me to the bed. To Melody—happy and healthy—and from the looks of it, ready to play.

Easing onto the mattress, I let out the breath I'd been holding.

"I thought..." Shaking the doomsday scenario from my head, I forced a smile. "It doesn't matter what I thought. How's it going, angel?"

Mel sat up, her grin losing a little luster with each second that ticked by.

When there was nothing left but the tiniest hint of a smile, she inhaled deeply and then asked, "Do you know how many people in the United States have diabetes, Christian?"

Scrubbing a hand down my face, I drew a blank. "Not exactly."

But I did know. To the exact number. I was just too wound up to pluck it from my thoughts.

Mel nodded slowly. "Let's find out."

Crawling over me to grab her phone from the nightstand, the sheet slid farther, revealing her perfect ass.

Draped over my lap, Melody hummed as she scrolled through her phone, her fingers in no particular hurry.

Forgetting the question, and my own name, I slid my palm from her thigh to the curve of her ass. "Fuck, baby, you look..."

"Twenty-nine million people, give or take." Triumphant, Mel pushed upright, straddling me.

My hands reflexively shot to her tits. "What?"

Gripping my jaw, Mel lifted my face to meet her gaze. "I said: twenty-nine million people in this country have diabetes."

I'm sure this was an important discussion, but right now, intellectual Mel wasn't who I wanted. Reversing our positions, I pressed her into the mattress.

"Good to know." Burying my face in the crook of her neck, I inhaled her sweet scent as I nibbled my way to her ear. "God, you smell good."

Exasperated, she drove her knuckles into my pecs. "Listen to me, Christian," she pleaded. "It's important."

Propping on my elbows, I peered down at her. Playful Melody had definitely left the building.

"What is it?"

Her brows drew together. "Do you think those people have friends?" Rolling her eyes when I didn't respond, she snapped, "The diabetics? Do you think they have friends? Do you think they go to college—have lives? Kids even?"

Scrutinizing her furrowed brow, I tucked a strand of hair behind her ear.

"Of course they do." I leaned in to kiss her but she turned her head. Unease warred with the desire slithering through my body as I gazed at her profile. "Mel, what's going on?"

"Do you care for me, Christian?"

She winced as the question tripped from her lips, her eyes never leaving the wall.

"Yes."

The answer spilled out before I had the chance to think about it. Because it was true. I *did* care about Mel.

She turned to me, hurt deepening the jade-green hue of her irises. "Then stop treating me like I'm some kind of broken toy. It's exhausting. And at some point, that's all you're going to see. The broken part." Tapping her chest, her voice cracked. "*I'm not broken.*"

Regret washed over me for making her feel . . . whatever way I'd made her feel.

Resting my forehead against hers, I pressed a kiss to her bottom lip. "I don't think you're broken, angel." Another kiss. "You're far from broken."

Mel slipped her arms around my neck, her fingers twisting in my hair. "Then stop treating me like I'm made of glass and show me." She wrapped her legs around my waist. "Show me right now."

"Be careful, angel." I smiled, rocking against her. "I said you weren't broken. Not that I wouldn't break you."

Mel's eyes lit up, like I'd given her a gift. "You can try."

"I think we both know what happened the last time you doubted me."

The heaviness in my chest lifted as I claimed her mouth. I knew in my gut there was more we should discuss. Whatever I'd done, I surely didn't want to repeat it. But right now, the need flaring in my belly was all consuming. The need to possess her. To protect her. To bury myself so deep in her body, she'd never go two days again without craving me.

I chided myself for the crazy inner dialogue.

Who knows where we'd be in two days, or two weeks?

What I did know is that I couldn't go another minute without feeling her sweet pussy wrapped around my dick.

"Damn, I can't wait to get inside you," I murmured, reaching for the box of condoms I'd stashed in her nightstand.

Mel's lids flew open, her mouth sliding from mine as I wrestled with the drawer.

"What are you doing?" she asked, gripping my arm.

"Condom."

She wiggled out from under me. "I'll get it."

A ripple of suspicion worked its way from my chest, creeping up my throat as Mel tried to pry my hand from the knob. But I didn't let go. If she thought I'd bolt if I saw her test kit or a needle, she was sadly mistaken.

"You don't have to hide things from me, Mel."

"I'm not hiding."

"Then let go of the knob," I challenged, pinning her in place with a stone cold gaze.

Reluctantly, she dropped her hand.

Out of the corner of my eyes I saw her chewing her lip as I rifled through the compartment. She turned beet red when I picked up the tiny silver massager.

Inspecting the toy, I couldn't keep from smiling. *This* is what she was hiding.

Smirking, I turned to face her. "Competition?"

The crimson flush spread to her chest, her rose tinted nipples puckering under my scrutiny.

"That's not . . . I don't . . ."

She winced when I pushed the button on top of the gadget and it purred to life.

"A do-it-yourselfer, huh?" I chuckled. "No wonder you haven't called me in two days."

"Don't be ridiculous." She tipped her chin. "You know I've had problems with that in the past."

Swirling the little vibrator over her nipple, I arched a brow. "The past? I'm not so sure about that." I dragged the toy down her body. "Did you use this last night?"

Pressing her lips firmly together, Mel glared at me but said nothing. If this was a war of wills, she'd lose, considering what I had in my arsenal.

She didn't protest when I spread her legs.

Rubbing the massager against her swollen clit, I waited until her eyes rolled back to pull it away.

Mel made a frantic grab for my hand, her nails digging into my skin. "Why are you stopping?"

"Because you didn't answer me." I tapped the massager against her tiny bud, never making contact for longer than a few seconds. "I can play this game all night. But I don't think you can, so answer my question."

Squirming, her hips jutted every time I grazed her engorged nub with the purring toy.

"I wonder if this thing has a higher setting," I mused. A wicked smile spread across my lips as I hit the button on top and the gadget responded with a louder buzz. "Looks like it does."

Mel grabbed my hand before I delved between her thighs, glaring. "Yes, damn it. I used it last night," she huffed. "Okay?"

Locking our gazes, I pressed a kiss to her knee. "Did you think about me?" My lips trailed to her inner thigh. "Don't lie."

My already pulsing cock throbbed painfully at the thought of her naked and writhing, the toy pressed to her drenched pussy as she called my name.

"Yes."

Squeezing my denim-clad shaft as I crawled off her, I paused when Mel gripped the back of my T-shirt.

"Where are you going?" Panic suffused her tone as she struggled to sit up.

Circling her wrist, I brought her hand to my lips and then kissed her palm.

"Anywhere you are, angel."

A pink flush stained her cheeks as I busied myself undressing.

I nudged the drawer shut with my knee when Mel leaned over to stash her little gadget.

"We're not done with that."

Her brows drew together. "We're not?"

Shaking my head, I stepped out of my jeans and then snatched the silk scarf from the arm of her desk chair.

Eyes darting from my rock hard cock to the scarf, she swallowed hard. "What are you going to do?"

Straddling her slim hips, I ran the silk through my fingers. "Nothing you don't want me to." When storm clouds brewed in her eyes, I cupped the back of her neck, caressing her cheek. "You know that, right?"

After a long moment she abandoned her grip on the toy and offered me her wrists. The girl never shut up, unless I really wanted her to speak. Then she was quiet as a church mouse.

Lifting one hand to my lips, I kissed her wrist.

"I'm not tying you up, baby" I eased on top of her, smiling. "Unless I have to. Now, close your eyes for me. I think you're going to like this."

I ran my thumb over the crease on her forehead where all her tension centered.

"Nothing you don't want me to do," I reminded her. "Not ever."

Without a word, Mel's lids fluttered closed. So compliant—in the bedroom, at least.

Warmed by the smile quirking her lips, I slipped the scarf over her eyes.

Her hands immediately flew to her face. "Christian . . ."

I tied the fabric so loosely, the silk nearly slid off the bridge of her nose.

"I'm right here."

Lowering my mouth to hers, I coaxed her into a passionate kiss. She relaxed, her fingers exploring my back and my shoulders. When her hand came to rest on my cheek, I leaned into her touch.

"Are you okay with this?" I asked, my voice a hoarse whisper. "Because if you're not—"

"I'm fine." A tentative smile curved her lips. "I mean . . . I think I'm fine."

"Don't think." I kissed her again. "You think too much already."

My gaze stayed on her face, appraising her every reaction as I sucked her nipple into my mouth. After working the rosy pebble to a stiff peak, I settled between her thighs.

If Mel had any reluctance at all, her body didn't get the memo. She was soaked.

"God, baby . . . you're so wet."

My tongue delved between her folds, teasing her entrance. She got sweeter every time I tasted her. Before I lost myself and took her along for the ride, I felt around for the little massager.

When the toy hummed to life, Mel's hand shot between her legs.

"No touching." I scored my teeth across her knuckles. "Are we clear?"

"Yes," she breathed, balling her fingers into fists at her sides. "Hurry, though."

For someone that spent her formative years watching mold grow, the girl had no patience.

I thrust two fingers inside her drenched pussy and she stopped twitching.

"You see, it all comes down to choices. Do you want this?" I swirled my tongue over her clit, flicking the tiny pearl. "Or this?"

I rubbed the tip of the little massager over her swollen bud and she groaned in approval.

Obviously, she trusted her battery-operated boyfriend more than she did me. But I was about to change that.

"I guess we've got a winner."

Stroking her deeply, I searched for her G-spot while I circled her clit with the vibrator.

"Oh, God . . . " she groaned loudly, "right there . . . don't stop."

My own release threatened and all I was doing was watching. I had no intention of stopping until I was buried to the hilt inside her warmth.

"Come for me," I rasped as I applied a little more pressure to the tiny bundle of nerves. "If you want my cock, you better let go." Trailing kisses to where my hand worked it's magic, I murmured against her skin, "You want my cock, don't you, baby?"

Her fingers curled into my hair. "Christian!"

I flattened the tip of the toy against her clit when I felt her inner walls tighten. The girl had a way of chasing away her own release if I didn't hold her down, and right now both my hands were busy.

As she rode out the second wave, moaning incoherently, I studied her.

Mine.

The word echoed in my head, drowning out anything that resembled a sane thought. Because it *was* insane, the draw I felt for Melody.

When she went limp, I pulled my fingers away and then grabbed the condom from the tangled sheets. She tensed as I ripped the foil packet with my teeth.

For a moment, I considered fucking her without removing the blindfold. But looking into those jade green eyes when she shattered wasn't something I could resist.

Settling on top of her, I slid the sash from her face.

"There she is." Gripping her thigh, I pulled her leg to my hip. "You ready for me, angel?"

I wasn't even sure what I was asking.

She smiled sweetly, wrapping her arms around my neck. "Yes, I'm ready."

Slipping inside her with one fluid thrust, I stilled, allowing her to set the pace. When her moans grew louder, I began to move. Determined to reach the finish line together, I pressed my forehead to hers, increasing the depth of my strokes until I met the end of her.

Crushing my mouth to hers, I cupped the back of her head to pull her closer as I spilled my release.

I held her there, swallowing all her moans, long after my body went limp. Because as long as we were joined, I could almost believe this contentment would last. That it was something more than a chemical reaction.

Logically, I knew it wasn't true. And I suspected Mel did as well. Hell, she even sported a tattoo that attested to the fact. Euler's Identity was a zero sum game.

There was no way around it. No manipulation that yielded a different result.

When you added all the numbers, the sum was always zero.

Reluctantly, I climbed off her and went to the bathroom to dispose of the condom.

Finding her curled on her side when I returned, the equation on her neck peaking from the curtain of her silky hair, I thought about leaving.

Then Melody twisted to look at me, her eyes soft and dreamy as she pulled the covers back so I could join her. Without thinking, I scooted beside her. Tucking her against my chest, I didn't think anymore about Euler's Identity or the future.

Tomorrow I'd wake up with Mel in my arms, and that's all that mattered.

Chapter 10

I pushed the food around my plate, mixing the stuffing and the corn into a neat pile. The pre-game coverage of the Cowboys matchup blared from the television in the adjoining room, replacing the Macy's Thanksgiving Day Parade broadcast.

Logan kicked my leg under the table. "Why aren't you eating, dude?" he asked, his mouth full of potatoes. "You miss your boyfriend?"

I shot him a glare and then mumbled an incoherent threat before dismissing him and returning to my food.

The dumbass hit a nerve, and he didn't even intend to.

I'd been trying to get Mel to spend Thanksgiving with me for the last week. She wasn't exactly forthcoming with the details, only telling me she had "plans."

Lily laid a plate of hot rolls on the table in front of me.

"Wow, Christian," she said, a wide smile curving her mouth. "I didn't know you were still seeing that girl from the college. You should've invited her for dinner."

I turned my scowl on Cameron.

He quit slathering butter onto his bread long enough to lift a shoulder. "What? I didn't think your dating habits were national security."

"They aren't." My glower melted to a tight smile as I addressed Lily. "Mel had plans tonight."

Plans...

I took a bite of lukewarm mashed potatoes to keep from answering any more questions.

"Well, it is Thanksgiving," Lily said, sinking into her chair with a frown. "People usually spend time with their families."

Taking her hand, Cameron brushed a kiss to her knuckles. "We are family, baby. Blood don't mean anything."

Lily gave Cam an indulgent smile that didn't reach her eyes.

I suspected the reason we were dining at this table instead of eating off TV trays in the game room had something to do with Lily. Growing up in one of the most prominent families in the country, she was used to grand traditions. Like sharing Thanksgiving with the governor and his wife at the Tennison's mansion in Dallas.

Lily never talked much about her estrangement from her parent's, but it was clear they weren't happy with her life choices.

Quitting business school in favor of completing her degree in fine arts was enough for the Tennison's to cut Lily off—financially, at least. But after Lily graduated and moved to Austin to "shack up" with her rock star boyfriend, the shit really hit the fan.

According to Cameron, Lily hadn't spoken a word to her mother, and her father's communication was spotty, at best.

I could totally relate. If my mom didn't put her foot down and insist I make the drive to College Station at least twice a year, I might never speak to my father again.

As if she could read my thoughts, Lily's eyes met mine over the table.

"You didn't want to spend Thanksgiving in College Station, Christian?"

With your family? She left that part out.

It was like the girl had telepathy or something.

"Cameron's right," I said, giving her a wink. "Family doesn't always mean blood. Besides, you're a much better cook than my mother."

Lily bit her lip, as if she wanted to say more. But she let me off the hook, steering the conversation to the Christmas tree lots that had sprung up overnight within a few miles of the house.

"We can't go get the Christmas tree right now, baby," Cameron whined, looking at his girl like she'd grown a third head. "The Cowboys are about to play."

Lily snorted. "Like that makes a difference. I've got a better chance of getting to the Super Bowl than Tony Romo."

Cameron's face paled at Lily's blasphemy. "We're nine and one," he choked. "Romo's not even playing. We've got to watch the game."

"I vote we get a tree," Logan piped up, shoveling stuffing onto his already teeming fork. "We can watch the Cowgirls anytime."

"You don't have a vote, asshat," Cameron growled, his hazel eyes narrowing.

"Yes, he does," Lily interjected, inching her way to Logan's side for moral support. "It's his Christmas tree, too."

Lily took Cameron's statement to heart about us being family. And from the looks of it she was determined to make our holidays as traditional as she could, given the band of misfits she had to work with.

Sean, quiet until now because he was too busy stuffing his face, tossed his napkin on the table and said to Lily, "Damn that was awesome, girl. You sure can cook."

A deep crevice etched her brow as she stared at the few small bones on his plate.

Sean's appetite was legendary. All you could eat buffets had been known to shutter their windows when they saw him walk through the door.

"Was the turkey dry?" Lily asked, wringing her hands. Before Sean could answer, she swung an accusing gaze at Cameron. "It *was* dry. I knew you left that damn bird in for too long."

"I did not," Cameron protested. "It's got a little button thing. I took it out as soon as it popped."

Logan snickered. "That's what she said."

In a flash, Cameron's hand shot out to slap the back of Logan's head. Logan responded by tossing his half eaten roll at Cameron's face.

Hunched over my plate, I hoped the impending melee would spare what was left of my dinner. Not that I was hungry anyway.

"The turkey was perfect," Sean cut in, prying Cameron's hand from Logan's collar. "I've got to save some room for supper at Aunt Melissa's." His smile widened. "But I've got time to help y'all pick out a tree before I go."

A satisfied smile curved Lily's mouth. "I'm going to get you a slice of my famous pumpkin pie for that, Sean."

Since Cameron wasn't through sulking, Lily leaned in to drop a kiss on his cheek on her way to the kitchen. When he captured her mouth instead, two minutes of smacking noises ensued, which did nothing for my queasy stomach.

Releasing Lily, Cameron waited until she was safely tucked in the kitchen before turning his white-hot gaze on Sean. "Way to have my back, asshole."

Sean barked out a laugh. "You know you're going to get the girl a tree." He smiled around his next swig of beer. "You're so fucking whipped, you can't deny her a thing. Don't even front."

Cameron shrugged, because really, what else could he do? Sean was only speaking the truth.

I managed to choke down a few more bites before excusing myself from the table.

Dropping onto the sofa, I turned my phone over in my hand as I watched the coverage of the Cowboys game.

Sighing in frustration, I gave in and tapped out a text to Mel. *Happy Thanksgiving.*

After waiting a few minutes for a reply that never came, I shoved the device in the pocket of my jeans so I wouldn't be tempted to send another message. As I retracted my hand from the worn denim, my fingers brushed against the metal fob with the single key attached.

I'd cajoled Mel into giving me her key a couple days ago under the guise of making her dinner. Not that I didn't intend to give it back. I wasn't turning into a stalker or anything.

Running my thumb over the metal grooves, I had my doubts.

"Game started yet?" Logan called as he entered the room. Joining me on the couch, he cast a suspicious eye in my direction. "What's that look about?

Ignoring his query, I pocketed Mel's key, smiling wide as Lily glided through the door with Cameron close behind.

"Did we decide on where to get that tree?" I said, shoving to my feet. "I'm ready whenever y'all are."

Chapter 11

Standing at the foot of the stairs leading to Mel's apartment, the five foot Douglas fir Christmas tree balanced on my shoulder, I cursed my stupidity. The lot had a delivery service, but made it clear they wouldn't be making any runs tonight. So I decided to go it on my own, telling the attendant to wrap it up and put it in the bed of my truck.

The guys didn't bat an eyelash, because of course, they'd assumed I was buying the tree for myself. Only Lily picked up on the obvious.

"That tree looks a little small," she'd noted, blinking up at me with doe eyes. "Unless you're going to put it in the bathroom or something."

She was right. The ceilings at my place were twenty feet high. But I'd already calculated the space Mel had in her tiny living room and the little Douglas fir I picked out was pushing it. Not to mention the problem I was now facing—getting the damn thing up the narrowest stairwell known to man. Gripping the bag of ornaments I'd picked up at Wal-Mart, I let out a sigh and then began my ascent. By the time I made it to Mel's landing, my hands were full of sap and I'm pretty sure I'd busted more than a couple of the delicate glass bulbs by cracking the bags against the walls in the narrow passageway.

Propping the tree against the wall next to Mel's door, I dug into my pocket to fish out her key. When soft noises drifted from inside the apartment, I stilled.

"Very late."

That's the vague answer Mel had given me when I'd asked her how long she'd be busy with her "plans."

Before I could think better of it, my fist shot out to bang against the flimsy wood.

The look on Mel's face when she found me on the stoop was like a punch to the gut.

"Christian." She hurried onto the welcome mat, pulling the door closed behind her. "What are you doing here?"

What the fuck *was* I doing here?

I glanced over Mel's flannel pajamas, messy hair, and freshly scrubbed face. Since my voice was trapped behind the lump in my throat, I motioned to the Christmas tree.

"I, uh," clearing my throat, I rubbed the back of my neck, "was going to surprise you. But I guess I was the one who was in for a surprise."

Mel's lips parted, then closed. When she tried again with the same result, I gave her a wry smile and then turned on my heel.

"Have a good night, Melody," I called, taking the steps two at a time.

The blood pounding in my ears wasn't loud enough to drown out the sound of her bare feet slapping the concrete behind me.

"Christian, wait."

Wait?

Not a chance. I sucked in a deep breath, resisting the urge to sprint. Mel's voice got closer, more insistent.

"Please!" Jogging to my side, she grabbed my arm. "You don't understand."

As she stood there, trying to catch her breath, the white-hot anger bubbling beneath my skin boiled over like a simmering cauldron.

"You're right, I don't understand. You told me you had plans." I flicked the sleeve on her worn T-shirt. "Obviously, you don't. If you wanted to be alone, you just had to tell me. I would've understood."

My fit of rage belied the point. Because I didn't understand. I wanted to spend the day with Mel. Wanted it so bad, I planned this little surprise so I'd have an excuse to steal a couple of hours with her when she was finished doing whatever it is she had to do.

Which, from the looks of it, was nothing at all.

Squeezing her eyes shut, Mel let out a frustrated sigh. "I do have plans. I just...I can't..."

Watching her struggle to let me down easy was more than I could bear. We'd made a silent vow to keep it casual, and I damn well intended to live up to it.

"I get the picture, angel." I shook off her grip. "Enjoy the tree."

Resuming my trek to the parking lot, Mel followed, struggling to match my brisk pace.

"There *is* no picture. I didn't want to ruin . . . I mean . . ." Clearly exasperated, her fingers circled my bicep as she ground to a halt. "Will you wait a fucking minute? I'm trying to talk to you."

Since ripping the girl's arm off wasn't an option, I complied. When she didn't say anything after a long moment, I let out a sigh.

"Mel, it's fine," I said evenly, hoping to appeal to her logical side so she'd stop trying to make up excuses. "You don't owe me an—"

Catapulting herself into my arms, her mouth crashed into mine with brute force. She thrust her tongue between my lips, seeking mine with wild abandon. Seizing control, I cupped the back of her neck and pulled her closer, letting her sweet taste wash away some of the anger.

When I couldn't sustain the kiss any longer, I stumbled back a foot, panting.

"Damn, angel." I ran my thumb over my bottom lip, checking for blood. "Is this the only way you know how to win an argument?"

"I wasn't the one arguing."

She was right, of course. As she tucked a fallen strand of hair behind her ear, I noticed the ink staining the side of her hand. Embarrassment filled the void where the anger had been. *Fuck.* She was graduating in two weeks and all I was thinking about was our nightly hook up.

I forced a smile as I ran my thumb over her kiss-swollen lips. "I know you've got to study. Give me a call when you want some company."

I pressed a quick kiss to her forehead and then turned to leave but she didn't release me.

"I already have company," she blurted.

Lily's pumpkin pie worked its way to the back of my throat. "You do?"

Toeing a groove in the sidewalk, she wouldn't look at me.

The sting from her rejection hurt like a bitch, but I managed to keep it light as I told her, "I'll let you get back to your guest then."

I barely took a step before her small voice rose behind me. "She's not a guest. She's my nana."

I spun around, confused. "Your nana?"

Squinting, Mel looked around, her gaze shifting to the trees, the parking lot, anywhere but my face. "She lives in a nursing home a few blocks from here. She's got a neurological disease—incurable."

Mel folded her arms around her waist, clutching the sides of her shirt before she continued. "Remember how I told you I used to work at a nursing home?" Her eyes met mine for confirmation and I nodded. "Well, I still do—fifteen hours a week. The pay is shit, but my discount just about covers what Medicare doesn't. They specialize in diseases like hers."

She tipped her chin, jutting out her bottom lip. "And just so you know, that's the only reason I turned down your invitation to go to The Parish. Nana can't speak, but she knows everything that's going on. I can't miss a day, unless she knows beforehand. Since you told me about the show that morning, I didn't have time to make plans. She would've been waiting for me."

Somehow during her speech, I'd closed the distance between us.

Molding my hands to her hips, I looked down at her, confused. "Why didn't you tell me?"

She shrugged, her usual posturing cast aside. "Because it's not pretty."

"Life ain't always pretty, angel. Its just life."

She nodded, a reticent smile curving her lips as she took a step back. "Since you're here now, would you like to meet her?"

Tiny rays of hope pushed aside the storm clouds in her expectant green eyes. I bent to kiss her, stealing a little piece of the sun.

"Of course I want to meet her." I gazed down at my beat-to-hell jeans and worn T-shirt. "I'm not exactly dressed to impress. But—"

She cupped my stubbly jaw, guiding my face to hers. "You're perfect."

Her smile was all the assurance I needed. That and the little peck she planted on my cheek. Before she could pull away, my fingers disappeared into her silky locks and I captured her mouth, softly this time.

She smiled as I nibbled away the last trace of cherry lip balm.

"Let's go," she said, taking my hand. "She's probably worried by now."

Mel's blond hair gleamed like a halo in the fading afternoon light as she pulled me along. An angel, just like I always proclaimed.

Mine.

Chapter 12

On our way up the stairs Mel babbled about her nana's condition. But as we approached the landing, the door loomed ahead like a portal into another dimension. I hadn't met a girl's family since my senior prom. And even then, I only stayed long enough for the chick's mother to fawn over my tux and snap a few pictures.

At the portal of doom, Mel turned to me, chewing nervously on her lip. "Did you get all that?" she asked.

I nodded dumbly, though I couldn't recall a damn thing she'd just said.

When Mel slipped inside, I gathered the tree and the ornaments, wondering how in the hell I ended up here.

The answer came to me in a rush when I entered the living room and spotted Mel kneeling beside a gray-haired woman in a clunky wheelchair.

I'd come here to give Mel a gift, but instead she was giving me something more valuable: a glimpse into her life.

Propping the Douglas fir in the corner, I waited while Mel whispered softly in her nana's ear. After prying the remote from the old woman's hand, which took some doing, Mel swung her gaze to mine, motioning me over with a slight jerk of her head.

Hesitantly, I closed the gap.

The old woman still hadn't moved, so all I could see was her profile as she stared straight ahead, clenching and unclenching her fists purposefully in her lap.

Tucking a finger under her nana's delicate chin, Mel guided the woman's face in my direction. Sparkling green eyes, worn by time and circumstances, met mine. The jade hue was a little dimmer, but the similarity was uncanny.

Drawn to the woman who had the eyes of an angel—just like her granddaughter—I took the final step and then dropped on one knee beside Mel.

"Nana, this is my friend, Christian."

The woman jerked slightly and Mel's irises lit like a thousand watt bulb, a wide smile breaking across her lips. I thought I knew all of her smiles, but this one I'd never seen.

My southern manners took over and I reached for her nana's hand. "Hello, ma'am."

The woman grasped my fingers with enough force to startle me. I'd met grown men with limper handshakes.

"I warned you," Mel said to me out of the corner of her mouth. "She can't control her grip. Especially when she's excited."

With a soft smile, Mel pried the woman's fingers from mine. "Christian, this is my na—this is Marina Sullivan."

Narrowing her gaze, her nana rasped, "M-mo." Closing her eyes, she took a gulp of air, then repeated in a clearer voice: "Mo."

Mel laughed at my confused expression. "She hates the name Marina, so everyone just calls her 'Mo.'"

There was no mistaking the smile in the old woman's eyes as she gazed up at her granddaughter. Something passed between them in the silence, and Mel snorted a laugh.

"Enough already," Mel quipped, shoving to her feet. "You're lucky I didn't tell him to call you 'Mrs. Sullivan.'"

Mo grunted, before shifting her eyes to the cup on the table.

With a mock sigh, Mel picked up the glass and then held the

straw to Mo's lips. "If you get drunk, I'm taking you straight home. That's your second glass of wine."

Mo took a sip and coughed, dribbling liquid on her chin.

Wiping the wine away without fanfare, Mel said, "Christian brought a tree. We're going to need your help decorating it, so lay off the sauce, okay?"

The faintest smile ghosted the old woman's lips as Mel turned her chair to face the wall where I'd placed the Douglas fir. Spotting the little tree, Mo jerked in her seat, her fingers working the fabric of her old gown furiously.

"She's excited," Mel whispered to me as I hauled to my feet. She smiled the softest smile she'd ever given me, then popped up on her tiptoes to peck my lips. "Thank you."

Mo's loud snort caught our attention. When it was apparent she was trying to choke out a few words, Mel rushed forward and lowered her head. After a long moment, she nodded, running her hand over her nana's silver tresses.

Mel straightened, her eyes moist and a pink flush staining her cheeks. "Um . . . I've got to go find something in my closet. Could you start setting up the tree?"

"Of course."

After cutting away the netting with my pocketknife, I set the small tree in the stand and then turned to Mo to gauge her reaction. Blinking at the tree, a fine mist gathered in her eyes.

She jerked when a loud crash sounded from the bedroom, her gaze darting to mine.

"I'd better go see what your granddaughter's gotten into." Mo's watery eyes locked on mine and she blinked twice. When I cocked my head, she repeated the gesture and then cut her eyes to the bedroom.

Two for "yes," one for "no."

Some of the information Mel recited about her nana when we were on our way up the stairs came back to me. I guess the two blinks were Mo's way of telling me to get my ass out of here and go help her granddaughter.

I gave her a quick nod and then did just that. Finding Mel on the floor of her bedroom in front of her closet sorting through a box, I knelt beside her.

"What are you doing?"

She turned to me in a panic. "I can't find the ornaments and the scrapbook," she babbled as she tossed item after item on the floor. "I know it's in one of these boxes . . . I just . . . I have to find it."

I touched her arm. "I bought ornaments. It's—"

"These are special." Her voice cracked. "I have to find them for her . . . I have to."

Spying a box tucked into a corner on the shelf above Mel's clothes, I stood up.

As I plucked the carton from its hiding place, I read the label on the side: *"Nana's things."*

Mel let out a relieved sigh as I placed the container on the floor. "Oh, thank God."

She ripped open the flap, the air leaving her body in a rush as she peered inside. I dropped onto my butt and watched as she carefully removed a worn box of ornaments. She lifted the lid and then ran her fingers lovingly over the little glass globes and other items.

I tucked a swath of blond hair behind her ear. "Why didn't you tell me, Mel?" She swung her gaze to mine, brows turned inward in confusion. "About your nana—you told me your family was gone."

In lieu of an answer, Mel removed a large scrapbook from the bottom of the container. Placing it on the floor between us, she opened the purple cover embossed with butterflies and flowers.

A black and white photo of a girl with Mel's eyes and smile stared back at me. She couldn't have been more than fifteen. From the age of the picture, I knew it wasn't Mel, though. It was Mo.

Under the image, the caption: "Once Upon a Time . . ." was hand written in calligraphy.

"I made this for her," Mel said softly. "So she wouldn't forget."

She turned the page, revealing a collage of photos, some very old and some that looked almost recent.

"This . . ." Mel choked, brushing her fingertips over the pictures.

"This is the woman I remember." Sniffling, she looked up at me. "The woman in these pictures *is* gone. But I'm sorry I didn't introduce you sooner. Because she's still an amazing person."

When Mel turned to the next page, I could feel the sadness wash over her like a tidal wave. She pointed to a photo of a man in his forties, perched on a stool in front of a keyboard on a small stage.

"This is my granddaddy." Her voice dropped to a near whisper. "He died of a heart attack seven years ago. Two years before nana got her diagnosis."

Shocked, I tipped forward for a closer look. "Was he a musician?"

When Mel didn't answer right away, I peered up at her. Tears rolled down her cheeks freely.

Wicking away the moisture with the back of her hand, she nodded. "Yes, but he wasn't famous or anything." She met my gaze, smiling. "Not like some people I know. He just filled in whenever a band was short a keyboardist." A proud grin replaced the sad smile. "He did work with the Eagles on the Hotel California album, though" She shrugged. "Along with a few other things. Taught me how to play the piano, too."

Scooting closer, I rested my chin on her shoulder. "You play the piano?" I chuckled. "And you didn't feel the need to share?"

She lifted her hand to cup my cheek. "So my stock's risen because I can pound out a couple tunes on the keyboard?"

Mel's stock rose every time she touched me. At the moment, she was worth more than my entire portfolio, sizable as it was.

She turned another page and stiffened, her back straight as a soldier.

I zeroed in on a photo of a woman who could pass for Mel's twin. "Who's that?"

"Harmony," Mel replied with a sigh. "My mother."

Harmony and Melody.

"Where is she?"

Mel's already rigid body turned stone still.

"Most of her is scattered off the shore near Padre Island." Mel dug through the container once again, producing a small velvet box. "But a little of her is right here." She flipped open the lid, revealing a tiny brass urn no larger than her palm. "She died when I was five. Drug overdose."

I wrapped an arm around her waist while her fingertip skated over the musical notes etched into the brass urn under her mother's name.

"I'm . . . I'm so sorry, angel."

Mel closed the velvet box with determination. "Don't be. I didn't really know her. My grandparent's raised me since the day I was born."

After a long moment, she turned her head slightly and our noses touched. "Go ahead." The glimmer was completely gone from her eyes. "I know you want to ask something else."

My lips brushed the corner of her mouth as I jumped to the next logical step on the journey she was taking me on. "What about your dad?"

She shuddered involuntarily. "I never met my father. Never even knew his name." A bubble of humorless laughter tumbled from her lips. "But then, I'm not sure my mom did either. From what I understand he was just some guy she hooked up with on one of my granddaddy's tours."

I pressed my forehead to her shoulder, wishing like hell I was anything but a musician. A guy like Melody's father who hooked up with women on the road and never even bothered to catch their names.

"I've never had a one-nighter, so you're going to have to tell me how it goes."

Melody's words from our first night rang in my ears. It was a miracle she didn't lure me to her house and set me on fire, leaving me to burn like the asshole she probably thought I was.

Before I could help myself, I offered up a truth of my own.

"You can have my dad if you want. He's a math professor." My lips ghosted the tattoo on her neck. "He'd love you. He doesn't care much for me, though. So if you want to visit him in College Station, you're on your own."

Mel twisted until we were face to face. "How could he not like you? You're such a—"

"'Disappointment' is the word he likes to use." Dropping my gaze to the shag carpet, I picked at the fibers. "But feel free to ad lib."

Cupping my cheek, she guided my face to hers. "I was going to say 'brilliant musician.'" She smiled the same smile she'd used on her nana. "But you're more than that."

After everything I'd just learned, it didn't seem right that she was offering me comfort. So I returned the favor the only way she'd let me. Slipping my fingers into her hair, I cupped her neck and pulled her toward me. My lips met the side of her mouth, then blazed a trail down her neck to her collarbone.

"You're amazing, Melody," I whispered.

Autumn clung to her skin, warming my insides. And I wondered if she smelled the same in the summer, or if sunshine emanated from her pores.

I realized right then—I really wanted to find out.

Hanging the last ornament on the tree, I turned to Mo and Mel for their approval. Perched next to Mo's chair, Mel nodded enthusiastically. "It's beautiful, Christian."

Mel's hand rested on her nana's lap, their fingers entwined. For the first time since I'd met Mo, her hands weren't clenching and unclenching. The only movement came from her thumb, stroking Mel's almost imperceptibly.

A baseball sized lump of emotion worked its way to the back of my throat at the sight of it.

Mo's face was frozen in a mask, but her eyes danced with delight. She blinked at me twice, her lips twitching as she tried to form a smile.

"I'm glad y'all like it," I said as I stood back to appraise the tree.

Scattered among the expensive ornaments I'd purchased were the one's Mel found in the box in her closet. A clay mold of her tiny handprint. A cardboard cutout in the shape of a Christmas tree, the red glitter nearly worn off. And my favorite by far, a golden angel kneeling in prayer with "Melody Rose Sullivan—1991" inscribed on the bottom.

"Turn on the lights!" Melody exclaimed, bouncing in her seat.

I found the end of the long strand of white bulbs and then plugged it into the extension chord.

"B-beaut—" Mo spluttered. Drawing her brows together in concentration, she swallowed hard and then choked out, "B-beautiful."

Melody beamed and I had to turn away. It was heartbreaking, the way she hung on any small word that left her nana's lips.

"What's the matter?" Mel asked, wrapping her arm around my waist. "You don't like it."

"I love it." I pressed a kiss to her temple, composing myself. "I thought you promised me some grub, though."

Melody laughed. "I hope you're not expecting much. I'm not really a good cook."

She glided away to turn Mo's chair toward the television. After a silent exchange, Mel put on a Lifetime Movie and then motioned for me to follow her to the kitchen.

Leaning a hip against the counter, I watched as Mel buzzed around the tiny cooking area.

Glancing at me while she stirred the gravy, she said, "You look like you've got something on your mind."

I cut my gaze to Mo in the other room. "What does your nana have—ALS?"

Given my limited interaction with the woman, Lou Gehrig's disease was the only thing that fit.

"It's in the same family of diseases. It's called PSP: Progressive Supranuclear Palsy." Mel smiled ruefully. "Say that three times fast."

"I've never . . ." I wracked my brain for any information and came up blank. "I've never heard of that."

"You will." Mel's eyes sparked with determination. "It's my second field of research. The protein I told you about at dinner that first night—Tau—that's why I study it. It's what causes PSP." She lifted a shoulder. "Or at least, that's the theory."

"They don't know what causes it?" A chill ran down my spine. "Is it . . . ?"

She blinked. "Hereditary?"

Gripping the counter, I nodded. The thought of Mel paralyzed and motionless, trapped inside her own mind, was enough to cut me off at the knees.

"No." The quick rush of relief evaporated when Mel added, "But there may be a genetic predisposition." A frown tugged at her lips. "Someday, we'll find out more. When there's enough money for adequate research. That's why I do the diabetes research. The school has funding for that since it's in the mainstream. PSP is an orphan disease."

"An orphan disease? What does that even mean?"

"Not enough people have it, and there isn't any known treatment."

The timer went off so Mel scooted away. Nose buried in the tiny oven, she poked the sad looking bird with a fork, frowning. "I don't think it's ready yet." She closed the door and turned to me sheepishly. "Like I said, I'm not a very good cook."

Wrapping her in my arms, I lowered my lips to her ear. "I'm not with you for you're culinary skills, angel."

She jerked her gaze to mine, shock painting her features.

From the beginning, we'd agreed we weren't a couple—that we weren't "with" each other in any permanent sense. From the look on Mel's face, my statement was a little too cozy for her liking.

Slipping out of my hold, she glided out of the room and left me standing there, cursing my stupidity.

After a few moments, she called my name.

I dragged my feet on the way to the bedroom, hoping she wasn't going to freak out and kick me to the curb for my awkward slip of the tongue.

When I walked through the door, Mel thrust the silk scarf in my hand.

I looked down at the swath of fabric. "What...?"

She shimmied out of her flannel pajamas and then offered me her wrists. "Tick-tock," she said, an amused smile tilting her pouty lips. "We've only got a few minutes before I have to take the turkey out of the oven."

Chapter 13

*P*acing the length of my bedroom floor, I paused when the bathroom door creaked open. Mel stepped out, tugging self-consciously at her short, black skirt. The plunging neckline on her teal blouse stopped somewhere short of indecent. *Maybe.* Since every thought in my head centered around ripping the garment from her body, I wasn't sure.

"Too much?" She slipped on a pair of black stilettos and then grimaced. "It's too much, huh?"

I caught her around the waist before she disappeared for another hour to mull over her wardrobe choices.

"You look," my eyes dropped to her cleavage, "amazing."

I made a mental note to keep Logan and anyone else over six-feet tall far away from her.

After our Thanksgiving Day celebration last week, Mel finally agreed to come to The Parish for a show. She even arranged to clear tomorrow's schedule. Which meant I'd have at least twenty-four hours to ravish her.

"Are you sure I look all right?" She bit her lip. "I feel naked."

Taking tentative steps to the full-length mirror, she scrutinized her reflection with a frown.

"If you were naked," I smiled at her reflection, "we wouldn't be leaving this house."

Why *were* we leaving the house? Bending her over the couch seemed like a much better option.

She sighed, stalking to the dresser to affix some dangly earrings. "You know what I mean. I'm more comfortable in jeans or a lab coat."

A wry smile lifted my lips. "I seem to remember doing some pretty dirty things to you in your lab coat."

She rolled her eyes. "Yeah, about that: who has fantasies of fucking someone in a lab coat?"

Me.

It didn't hurt that she was handcuffed to the bed at the time. Or that she was wearing her special red stilettos.

From the look on her face, I'd lost a couple moments recalling that fantasy.

"Freak," she muttered, shaking her head.

"Right back at you, angel."

She pushed me away when I determined we had about nineteen minutes before we had to leave. Plenty of time to show her how freaky I really was.

"You don't understand. I'm trying to fit in," she grumbled. "It's bad enough that I have nothing in common with these people."

"These people are my family." Defensiveness crept into my tone. "And you've never even met them."

She sighed. "I didn't mean anything. *I'm* the freak. And not in a good way. I don't fit."

"That's not true." Brushing the hair off her neck, I kissed her shoulder. "You fit."

We fit.

I stopped short of that little admission.

"But—"

"No 'buts,'" I squeezed her ass, "except this one. I don't know what you're so keyed up about. I go to your study groups."

"Study groups are fun." Cringing, she squeezed her eyes shut. "See, that's what I mean. That's the kind of shit that pops out of my mouth. 'What do you do for fun, Melody?' 'Oh, I study diseases. You?'" She groaned. "I'm sure that will go over really great with your friends."

Leading her to the couch, I took a seat, coaxing her onto my lap. "These aren't just any friends. I told you, they're family. And they're going to love you."

Love. My stomach twisted as the word hung in the air. Absorbed in her thoughts, Mel didn't respond to my tension.

"If you say so." She swallowed, her mouth twisting like she tasted something sour. "I just don't want people . . . you know . . . to wonder why we're seeing each other."

I tilted her chin and she reluctantly met my gaze. "The only thing my friends are going to wonder is what you're doing hanging out with me."

She smiled with no confidence. Even as I lowered my mouth to hers, kissing her with all the passion I could muster, trepidation spilled off her in waves.

I smiled against her lips. "Time to go."

Guiding her to the door, she lagged behind as though she faced imminent execution.

"Hold on," I said, doubling back to snatch her scarf from the bedpost. "In case you get cold." I winked, slipping the soft fabric around her shoulders. "Or horny."

She snorted a laugh, straight from her belly. "I am *not* going to fuck you in the bathroom at The Parish." She narrowed her eyes. "You do know that, right?"

"Of course not." Resting my hand on her luscious ass, I squeezed. "The bathroom is way too crowded. But there's always the dressing room."

"Dude, your girl is a hoot." Cameron nudged my shoulder. "Why didn't you bring her around sooner?"

I smiled tightly, my eyes never leaving Mel and Lily, dancing a few feet from the VIP section. My stomach twisted when I noticed them weaving through the crowd, headed for the bar. *Again.*

By my count, this made shot number three. Plus the two beers she had in the dressing room before the show.

For me, that was nothing. For Mel? I wasn't sure. She was too nervous to eat before we came, so my anxiety catapulted straight through the roof when she started pounding shots.

Unable to stand it any longer, I shot to my feet. "I'm going to check on the girls. Be right back."

Cameron grabbed my arm. "Whoa . . . hold on a minute."

"What the fuck?" I snapped, shaking off his hand. "I said I'd be right back."

"Don't be stupid," he said evenly. "Send Seth. That's what we pay him for. You might get mobbed if you hit the main floor."

The security guard in question stood in front of the VIP area, his thick arms crossed over his chest.

"I'll take my chances."

Cameron groaned, but followed me nonetheless.

"Dude, what's your problem?" He fell into step behind me as we elbowed our way into the crowd. "You're the one who's always talking about security. All these people just saw us on stage an hour ago."

Waving off Cameron's warning, I reached the bar in time to find Mel and Lily clinking glasses.

Wrapping my arm around Mel's hip, I leaned close to her ear. "Having a good time?"

She looked up at me with unfocused eyes.

"I'm having a *greeeat* time," she purred. "Where have you been? I haven't seen you in *aaages.*"

Rising to her tiptoes, she planted a sloppy kiss on my mouth. Or near my mouth.

"I need another drink." Eyes hooded, she rocked against me. "Buy me a drink, rock star, and I promise you'll get lucky tonight."

"Is that right?"

Sliding my fingers into the damp hair at the nape of her neck, I pressed a kiss to her lips.

If distracting Mel was my goal, she turned the tables on me. Her tongue swept into my mouth, twisting and tangling around mine for what seemed like forever. The alcohol mixed with her unique taste, enlivening my senses.

My eyes popped open when I felt an insistent tap on my shoulder. I twisted to find Lily glaring at me with mock irritation.

"You need to quit pawing my dance partner." She slapped my chest with an uncoordinated hand. "We're not done yet."

My hearty laugh died when Lily wiggled between us, forcing another shot into Mel's hand.

Taking a sniff of the clear liquid, Mel's brows shot to her hairline. "What octane is this?"

"That's tequila—fully leaded." Lily giggled at Mel's skeptical expression. "You've never tried tequila? Where you been hiding, girl —under a rock?"

"Kind of." Mel took another whiff.

Grabbing a saltshaker, Lily continued, "I used to work in a bar. There's a right way and a wrong way to do a shot of tequila. Let me show you how it's done."

Mel peered up at me as Lily forced Cameron onto a barstool. "What are they going to do?"

"Watch." Wrapping my arms around Mel's waist, I tucked her back to my chest. The longer this little show went on, the more time I'd have to either down Mel's shot, or hide it.

Lily snagged the lime from the rim of the glass and waived it in Cameron's face. "May I?"

He smiled. "Sure, darlin'. I'm game."

Lily slipped the fruit between Cameron's teeth, drawing the attention of a few rowdy patrons nearby.

Body shot! Body shot! Body shot!

The chorus rang out as the revelers clapped and hooted, their cries drowning out the music pouring from the speakers above the bar.

Eager to comply, Lily grabbed the shot of tequila while simultaneously gripping the front of Cameron's jeans. Catching her wrist, he shook his head emphatically.

Once upon a time, Cameron not only enjoyed a woman retrieving a shot from the waistband of his jeans, he encouraged it. But Lily was his girlfriend. And a picture of her diving head first into his crotch was not an image he wanted circulating.

Prying the glass from her hand, Cameron held it gingerly between two fingers. Lily pouted, but in this case it did her no good. The boy might be whipped, but he wasn't that whipped.

Since Cameron wasn't budging, Lily put in some extra effort when she licked her wrist and applied the salt. Cam's eyes glazed over as her tongue darted out to retrieve the granules.

When she was sure she had his full attention, Lily launched herself at him.

Everyone cheered as she crushed her lips to his. Oblivious to the cameras memorializing the moment, Cameron devoured her mouth. It took a good minute for Lily to pull away with the rind between her teeth.

Caught up in the moment, I clapped along with everyone else until I felt Mel grip my arm.

Eyes wide, she blinked up at me. "I want to do that." She licked her lips. "Right now."

I slanted my gaze to the shot dangling from her fingertips. "How many of those have you had, angel?"

Ignoring the question, Mel pinned me against the bar, a devious smile curving her lips. My wariness faded as she coaxed the fruit into my mouth. She looked totally fucking hot, clumsily licking the salt from her skin. And I wasn't the only one who noticed.

After Cameron and I arrived, more and more people wandered to the bar. And since we had no security to hold them at bay, I got a clear shot of the dude checking out Mel's ass. I was about to stand, when she downed the shot.

Then her mouth was on mine, and her fingers were in my hair. I fought valiantly, but she won the battle, her nimble tongue prying the lime wedge from my teeth with little effort.

Stumbling out of my arms, she took a wobbly bow in deference to the cheers ringing out around us. The asshat who'd been staring at her ass was now looking directly at her tits, a lascivious grin on his mug.

Mine.

"Come here," I rumbled. "I'm not done with you."

She yelped as I cupped the back of her neck, my mouth descending on hers possessively. As my thumb caressed the soft, dewy skin at the hollow of her neck, the background noise fell away, my world reduced to the faint beat of her heart thrumming beneath my touch.

Mine.

Hearing Logan's loud chuckle, I slid my lips from Mel's. Leaning against the bar with Seth the security guard at his side, Logan shot me a shit-eating grin.

"I can see why Christian's been keeping you under wraps," he said to Mel. "You're a wild thing, aren't you?"

Instinctively, my fingers dug into the curve of Mel's waist. "I haven't brought her around because she's busy. I told you she's a grad student. She studies—"

Mel slapped my arm in a playful yet decisive gesture. "Nobody wants to hear about *thaat.*"

Ignoring Logan completely, Mel pecked me on the lips and then lurched toward Lily. The two of them nearly fell into a heap, giggling when they bumped heads. I caught Mel's elbow to steady her, but she shimmied free.

"We're going to dance," Lily announced, grabbing Mel by the hand. "See y'all later."

Mel shrugged as Lily hauled her away. Arm in arm, they teetered toward the main floor. My smile evaporated when the crowd pushed in around them.

"What's up your ass, Wikipedia?" Logan took a long draw from his beer, eyeing the dance floor. "I wouldn't be wearing a frown if I was taking Melody home tonight."

A flash of heat shot through me. Jealousy? I'd never felt it. But at the moment, ripping Logan's arm off and beating him with it seemed like an option.

"You're not taking her anywhere." My response was somewhere between a growl and a roar. "And quit looking at her like you want to make her a meal, dude. I'm fucking serious."

Pausing with the bottle halfway to his lips, Logan's brows drew together. "Chill, man. You're starting to sound like this one over here." He hitched a thumb over his shoulder at Cameron. "There's plenty of fine ass to go around. Y'all don't have to worry about me cutting in on your action."

Cameron and I exchanged a look of indignation. I'm guessing he didn't like having his girlfriend referred to as "fine ass" any more than I did.

Girlfriend . . .

The word sounded foreign. Other people had girlfriends. People who didn't know any better. Ready to mount a protest, I spotted Mel gyrating on the dance floor. She crooked a finger at me, her brilliant smile flashing under the pulsing lights. Suddenly, I didn't care about the title, as long as the word "my" was in front of it.

Waving off Seth's attempt to keep me in my spot, I edged into the crowd in search of my girl.

"There she is." I took Mel's hand and spun her around. "How's it going, beautiful?"

God, she *was* beautiful. And flushed.

Her forehead wrinkled. "I'm a little thirsty. It's hot in here, right?"

It was hot, but not overly so. And thirst was one of the warning signs of diabetes. Did that apply to all diabetics or just those who weren't diagnosed?

Taming the wild thoughts ricocheting around my head, I cupped Mel's cheek. She was soaked, the back of her neck slick with sweat.

"You don't look good. I think it's time to go."

"No, Christian. I'm having a good time. I feel . . ."

My chest tightened as I watched her fumble to find the word. "You're not well. We're going."

Overhearing my comment, Lily spun around, cocking her head at Mel. "Are you all right, sweetie?"

"I'm . . . I'm fine," Mel stammered. "I'm fine."

The last time she told me she was fine her blood sugar was fifty-three.

Picturing every catastrophic scenario, I shifted my gaze to Lily and said, "We're leaving. Mel's sick."

The minute I said it, I realized my mistake. Words like "sick" didn't exist in Mel's vernacular when it came to her diabetes.

She glared at me.

"I mean, she's not feeling well," I amended. "Too much tequila."

Lily nodded, wordlessly falling into place behind Mel as I pushed our way through the crowd.

When we exited the dance floor, Mel pumped the brakes. "Christian," she bit out. "I said I was fine."

Lily looked between us. "Honey, if you're sick—"

"I'm not sick!" Mel roared. Pressing her lips together when she noticed Lily's alarmed expression, she mumbled, "I'm sorry. I'm just . . . I'm not sick."

"She's fine," I interjected "She's a—"

I stopped myself a second before the "D" word tripped past my lips. Taking a deep breath, I forced a smile before lying through my teeth.

"Mel just got over a cold. Isn't that right, angel?" Mel nodded, staring at her toes. "So I think we're going to call it a night."

We stopped at the bar long enough for Mel to give Lily a hug and offer a slurred good-bye to the rest of my crew.

She didn't say anything when I entwined our digits and led her away, but I could feel the anger swirling around her like a cyclone.

Once we entered the maze of hallways in the back of the club, Mel shrugged off my grip. Irritation tensed my jaw when she lagged behind, but I couldn't decide if I was mad at myself, or at her.

Pushing the back door open, my head cleared as soon as I inhaled the crisp, autumn air. When I turned to offer some kind of explanation, Mel was headed in the other direction, stumbling toward the alley leading to the front of the building.

I reached her in four quick strides, catching her around the waist. "Where are you going, baby? The cars over—"

"Don't call me baby. I'm not a baby." She wiggled out of my hold. "I'm getting a cab."

My temper flared, even though I knew she had every right to be annoyed.

"Melody," I took her elbow, "you're fucking trashed. Stop acting stupid and—"

"Stupid?" She rose to her tiptoes, because, apparently she needed the extra few inches to make sure her ear-splitting shriek caught my attention. "You're calling me stupid?! I may be drunk, but I'm not stupid! You just embarrassed me in front of everyone!"

"I didn't—"

"Yes, you did!" Moisture welled in her eyes. "I was just . . . I wanted to fit in. And you..."

Her thought trailed off as she looked at me, a solitary tear dancing on her eyelash.

I blew out a breath. "Look, I was just worried, okay? You didn't eat. And the booze—"

"You think I don't *knooow* about booze?" She narrowed her unfocused eyes. "I've been a diabetic since I was six years old." She held up seven fingers—which would have been funny if she wasn't so damn mad. "I've even dranken before." She shook her head. "I mean, I've even drank before."

I rubbed the back of my neck, playing the nights events over in my head. Mel's cheeks were no longer flushed and she didn't appear to be in any distress.

"Maybe I overreacted."

"That's the *proooblem*, Christian." She lurched, fisting my T-shirt as she fought for balance. "I didn't ask for your help. You're as bad as Mitch." Stumbling to the wall, she leaned against the bricks.

Anger flared as I closed the gap between us. Tucking a knuckle under her chin, I forced her gaze to mine.

"What's Mitchell got to do with this?"

"Not a damn thing since I stopped doing him." She hiccupped, and then she amended, "*Dating* him. Since I stopped dating him."

Grinding my molars, I grabbed her hand. "Come on; we're going."

"I want a cab," she whined, stumbling along behind me.

"Too bad." I shot her a glare. "I want a lot of things. That doesn't mean I'm going to get them."

At the moment, the thing I wanted most was the image of her and Mitchell scrubbed from my brain.

Yeah, that wasn't going to happen either.

Chapter 14

*H*unched over my Froot Loops, I pushed the soggy cereal around the bowl. Mel's breakfast of choice—scrambled eggs with a side of turkey bacon—sat untouched on a plate in front of the barstool next to mine.

I made the meal as a peace offering. Apparently I'd suffered some kind of short-term memory loss last night at The Parish. I *knew* Mel wasn't in any danger. Hell, I'd made it my business to find out everything I could about diabetes in the last month. Every medical journal I'd read stated clearly that overindulging in alcohol, on occasion, posed no serious threat to a stable diabetic.

But even with that knowledge, I couldn't help myself. And that was the real problem.

If I'm honest, I worried about Mel all the fucking time, and it wasn't limited to her diabetes. If she was late coming home from the library, I pictured her in a ten-car pile up on the freeway. If she got wrapped up in her studies and didn't call, I sent her a text to find out where she was.

My phone, which I largely ignored before I met Mel, was now a permanent appendage. And we weren't even together.

Were we?

Taking another bite of cereal, a sinking feeling washed over me as I gazed around the room. Mel's stuff was everywhere. Neat little piles of textbooks on the table. A container of her favorite hot chocolate next to the coffee pot. Even the fucking recycling bin had more empty cans of diet soda than beer bottles.

Stalking to the sink, I dumped what was left of my breakfast in the drain. The brightly colored rings slid down the river of milk and around the mug with the UT emblem on the front.

Begrudgingly, I turned on the faucet and then squirted some soap on the inside Mel's cup. The damn girl was content to splash some water over the damn thing and call it a day. If I didn't wash it for her . . .

I stopped scrubbing and placed the mug back in the sink.

Still grappling with my thoughts, I jerked my gaze to the archway when Mel walked in, clutching an armful of folded laundry to her chest.

"I made you something to eat," I said as I picked up her coffee cup and resumed my scouring. "Do you want hot chocolate or coffee?"

When she didn't answer, my jaw ticked in irritation.

I let out a sigh as I turned to the coffee pot. "Coffee or hot chocolate, Melody?"

"Neither."

I spun around, zeroing in on the pile of clothes disappearing into the plastic garbage bag in her hand.

"What are you doing?"

Expecting to see fire shooting from her eyes when she looked up, I was stunned when she gave me a sad smile. "I'm leaving, Christian."

I leaned my butt against the counter, gripping the beveled edges to keep from falling over.

"Leaving where? You've got the morning off."

My near growl caught her attention, and she sank onto the barstool in front of her plate.

"I'm going home." Averting her bloodshot eyes, she let out a staggered breath. "I'm sorry if I embarrassed you last night. I . . . I wasn't myself."

The remnants of my breakfast threatened to creep up my throat and join their friends in the sink. She actually though this was *her* fault.

Frustrated, I rubbed the back of my neck. "Listen, Mel, I um . . . I overreacted last night. I was just—"

"I know." She cringed, squeezing her eyes shut tight. "You didn't want me to get sick."

"Well, yeah, that was part of it."

After I figured out that Mel wasn't going to go into some kind of sugar shock, I spent the rest of the night tossing and turning, images of her and Mitch the Bitch bouncing around in my head.

Taking a seat on the stool next to her, I blurted, "Why didn't you tell me about Mitchell?"

Mel cocked her head. "What about him?"

Folding my arms over my chest, I scrutinized her with a narrowed gaze. "That y'all used to date?"

"I told you I've known him for a long time."

"You also told me he was your *lab partner*. I didn't ask any questions because he doesn't seem like your type. I never thought . . ." I blew out a breath. "Was it serious?"

She shrugged half-heartedly. "Not really. I guess he wanted it to be. Which is why I broke up with him. I thought he treated me the way he did because of his research background."

My back stiffened, both from her words and her apathy. "How did he treat you?"

"Like a project," she replied in the same dull monotone. "Always checking my food, or reminding me to take my shot. Eventually, he wouldn't even touch me." She chuckled, then looked down at her hands. "Unless it was to test my sugar."

"I would never—"

Mel's eyes met mine, resignation darkening the brilliant jade hue of her irises.

"Yes you will. You already did." She took a deep breath to fortify her reserves, and then continued, "I try to go about my life and act like everything's fine. Like I'm normal. I tried to be normal last night.

To prove to you that I could fit in." She wobbled to her feet. "But I guess I can't. And I don't want to be *that* girl."

I took her hand before she did something stupid, like bolt. "What girl?"

Brows drawn inward, she gazed at our entwined digits. "The girl I've always been—the sick girl." Peering up at me, a watery smile curved her lips. "When I was twelve, I spent an entire week in the hospital after a slumber party. A stupid slumber party where I ate too much ice cream and pigged out on gummy bears."

"Why would—?"

"Because I wanted to be like everyone else." She frowned at the admission. "When I was really young, I used to skip my shots every now and then, just to see if I was cured."

"You were a kid. Kids do stupid shit." I managed to chuckle over the dry lump in my throat. "If it makes you feel any better, I once calculated the wind current and jumped out of a second story window with some wings I made out of a tarp." I lifted my arm. "Broke my ulna. Bone came right through the skin."

Running her fingertip along the raised edges of the scar, she murmured, "But you healed and I never will." A tear slid down her cheek and landed on my skin, burning straight through to my bone marrow. "I didn't think . . . I mean . . . I thought you and me, we'd have some fun, and that would be that."

"You're not having fun?" I leaned in low, searching for her eyes. "I'm having fun."

She pinned me with her jade green gaze.

"Were you having fun last night?" she asked, her bottom lip quivering. "Did you enjoy getting on your iPad to see if I was going to have some kind of seizure?"

"You saw that?"

She rolled her eyes. "I was drunk, not blind. Although, prolonged abuse of alcohol in diabetics can lead to blindness."

Throwing in that fun fact, she slipped her hand from mine and then shuffled to the dining room table to gather her books.

"I was a fucking idiot, Mel." I stole behind her, pressing my chest to her back. "I was worried for nothing. I know that now."

She spun around, leveling her most serious gaze on me. "About the alcohol, maybe. But there are other things. I didn't exactly win the genetic lottery. What if I get sick—really sick?" She swallowed hard, fighting the tears welling in her eyes. "That might put a kink in things, don't you think?"

When I didn't answer, she turned and continued to shove her books into her backpack. "I know I told you I don't believe in love. But that's not exactly true. What I don't believe in is happily ever afters. Not for myself, at least."

Pushing me out of the way, she returned to the breakfast bar and then finished packing her clothes. I followed, as if my feet had a mind of their own.

"What are you saying, Mel?"

Hoisting the tote over her shoulder, she shifted away from me.

"That you're a sweet guy. I didn't expect you to be a sweet guy. I didn't expect . . . hell, I didn't expect anything, Christian. It's time to stop pretending this is anything more than it is, so you can get back to your life."

"What do you mean: get back to my life?" Prickling at her suggestion, I added sarcastically. "I've been living my life, baby. In case you haven't noticed."

Mel's eyes raked me over like we just met. Like I was the guy in the picture hanging on the wall at the burger joint where she used to work.

"What about the parties and the clubs? All the things you used to do instead of hanging out at the library."

Before Mel, clubs and parties *were* the diversion. A place to go instead of the library. But even if I told her all the things spinning around in my head, the way I felt this very moment, it wouldn't stop the inevitable. Someday soon, when my feelings faded, I'd hurt her. Much worse than she was hurting now.

Shoving my hands deep in my pockets, my fingers grazed the

silver fob. Hooking my thumb in the ring, I pulled her key from its hiding place.

"I guess you're right, angel," I said thickly, pressing the small piece of metal into her palm. "I can't hide out in the library forever." The lie tumbled out with surprising ease. "Good luck with everything."

I'll miss you.

Biting my tongue, I took a step back, adopting a casual posture while Mel stared down at the key in her hand. When she finally met my gaze, I braced myself for whatever she was going to say.

Lay it on me, angel. I deserve it.

Though I knew I was doing all this for her own good, I still felt like shit. I wanted Mel to rage at me, kick my ass for letting her go. But instead she rushed forward, her body molding to mine like she owned it.

Cupping my face in her small hands, she smiled, tears streaming down her face unchecked. "Good luck to you too, rock star."

And then she was gone, her Chucks squeaking against the tile floor as she bounded down the hall.

When the door clicked shut behind her, I waited for the relief. I spent a good minute just standing there, expecting the sky to open up and sunshine to warm my face.

But the farther away Mel got, the colder I felt.

I sprinted for the door, chasing something I had no right to chase.

"Mel, wait a minute!" I yelled, stumbling onto the porch.

The whine of her engine drowned out my voice as I hurried down the stone steps. I made it to the curb in time to see her pull out of the driveway.

With a lump the size of a boulder lodged in my throat it was hard to get the words out. But I managed.

"I love you."

It wasn't a scream to the heavens. Just a tiny stitch in time. *Today*, I loved her. That was the truth. As fleeting as the feeling might be, Melody deserved the words, even if she couldn't hear them. She also deserved a man who'd be able to say them without wincing.

Shoving my hands in my pockets to ward off the chill that slithered over my skin, I headed up the path, leaves crumbling under my feet.

In a couple of weeks, winter would descend and sweep away the fall, along with the girl that smelled like autumn. Logic told me it was true. But the invisible fingers wrapped around my heart gave me pause. In reality I knew they didn't exist, anymore than the notion that love was a permanent state of mind.

But if that were the case, why couldn't I breathe?

Chapter 15

As I waited in the dressing room for the rest of the band, I gingerly opened the white envelope with the burnt orange seal in the corner. In the seven days since Mel had walked out of my life, I'd avoided anything that might disrupt the scab on the wound she left behind.

Since I'd also given up checking my email, going to the library, and showering unless completely necessary, I didn't find the invitation for her graduation until this morning.

The event was taking place tonight at the Erwin Center, but I already knew that.

Pulling the heavy parchment from the envelope, I ran a finger over the embossed school seal featured proudly at the bottom.

The cushions sank under Cameron's weight as he plopped on the couch next to me.

"What's that?" He propped his feet on the worn table before snatching the invitation from my grasp. Glancing over the loopy inscription, he smiled. "Impressive. Does this mean you're going?"

"We're not seeing each other anymore," I snapped, plucking the card from his hand. "Why the hell would I go?"

"Dude, stop being so defensive. I just thought you were into the chick. My bad."

"I was." *I am.* "She's the one that broke it off."

"That's probably the best thing," he eyed me suspiciously, "since you let her."

Sliding a hand through my greasy hair, I gripped the strands at the base of my neck. "I didn't 'let her' do anything. If a girl wants to jet, it's her choice."

"Keep telling yourself that, bro." Cameron chuckled. "We'll see how it works out for you."

It took all my restraint not to wring his neck. A few months ago, Cameron would've been urging me to join him at a strip club to get over this little bump in the road. Not encouraging me to prolong the agony.

"Let me ask you something, Dr. Phil," I said dryly. "Have you ever thought about what's going to happen when something goes south with Lily?"

The motherfucker chuckled. He actually laughed.

"*When?* That's mighty cynical." He patted my knee. "But, no, I don't think about that. It's not going to happen."

"*Today*—it's not going to happen *today*."

I shook my head. Reasoning with people like Cameron never got me very far, but hey, I was willing to try.

Crossing my arms over my chest, I let out a sigh and then began, "Over fifty percent of marriages end in divorce. And I'd venture to say the other fifty percent are just like my parents. They stay together out of habit. We're not even talking about people just casually dating, so—"

"Is that what y'all were . . . casual?" Cameron cocked his head, truly interested in my response.

Mel and I spent every day together. Casual wasn't a word I'd use. "No, we weren't casual, but—"

"'But' nothing." His hazel eyes darkened with irritation. "I've heard all your statistics and bullshit theories." I raised a brow and he softened. "Let's say it's all true. Every word of it. I still want you to think about one thing."

Tamping down my exasperation, I waited for whatever inane argument Cameron was about to make.

"Have you ever thought about how many bands out there—good bands—struggle to get a song on the charts?" he asked, a smug smile curving his lips. "Millions."

Rolling my eyes, I wondered where the train went off the tracks.

"What's your fucking point, Cameron?"

Please, God, let there be one.

"We did it." Gazing around at the framed magazine covers and other accolades, Cameron shrugged, and then turned that smug smile back in my direction. "That one in a million thing? Ain't no step for a stepper. You just gotta believe."

Some of Lily's brainpower must've rubbed off on the dude, because he was actually making sense. Either that, or I was grasping at straws.

When Cameron arched a brow, waiting for my response, I conceded, "Well, yeah, I guess we did."

"So if that's the case," he continued, settling back against the cushions. "What makes you so fucking sure you can't make a go of it with Mel?"

"I didn't say we couldn't make it. I said the odds—"

Cameron rolled his eyes in exasperation. "What the fuck do the odds have to do with it? Even if the odds were ninety percent that Lily and me would blow up, I'd take the bet. You know why?" I shook my head, even though I suspected I already knew what he was going to say. "Because one day with Lily is worth the price. Even if you told me there were a thousand days of misery in my future, I'd take those twenty-four hours."

I blanched inwardly when I thought about the last seven days. If I had to endure a thousand more, I wouldn't make it.

"That's you," I said quietly. "This time next month, I won't even remember what she looked like."

Cameron studied my lying face for a moment before slowly rising from his seat. "Well, there you go." He leaned down to pat my shoulder, a smirk tilting his lips. "What's her name is obviously not the right chick for you or it wouldn't be that easy."

"Her name is Melody," I grumbled. "And there is no 'right chick' for anyone."

"Whatever you say."

With a skeptical eye, I watched Cameron stroll to the fridge, looking for any chinks in his armor. Any sign that he was fooling himself. I mean, the guy used to bang groupies two at a time and party his face off until dawn almost every night.

"Do you miss it?" I blurted, regretting the question when he spun around with that carefree smile.

"Miss what?"

"Everything. The parties, the clubs." I raised a brow. "The threesomes."

He barked out a laugh. "Have you *seen* my girl? Fuck, dude, there's nothing to miss. I got it all."

Closing my eyes I let my head fall to the back of the couch. Cameron reclaimed his seat and then knocked me with his elbow. "You want some Chinese? I'm placing an order."

My stomach turned at the thought of food. "I'm good."

And now I was flat out lying. I wasn't close to being good. I hadn't had an hour of good in seven days.

The door swung open and I threw my arm over my face, hoping whoever it was would leave me alone until rehearsal.

I jerked, my eyes popping open when a boot met my shin.

Chase Noble, Cameron's brother, stood over us, glaring. I'm assuming from the way Cameron was rubbing his leg, his shin got the same treatment.

"This place gets filthier every time I come in here," Chase complained. "The cleaning crew is starting to complain. Get off your asses and grab a trashcan."

Since Chase owned the club, and was technically our boss, his look of reproach should've carried more weight. But I'd known the guy since I was fifteen.

Reluctantly, Cameron and I pushed to our feet and began to tidy up, while Chase took a seat at the desk in the corner.

"Did the band ever agree on which charity they wanted to sponsor for the Christmas event?" he asked offhandedly as he sorted through some mail.

Cameron examined the contents of a pizza box, grimacing. "Just so long as it's not breast cancer again. We don't need to give Logan another opportunity to provide his 'free examinations.'"

Chase leaned back in the rickety chair, crossing his long legs at the ankle.

"We raised fifty grand that night," he said, leveling a wry smile in Cameron's direction. "And those 'exams' Logan offered? They weren't free. The women all contributed a sizable donation to participate."

Cameron wrinkled his nose. "So you don't care if Logan gropes women for money?"

Chase laughed. "Before Lily, you fondled plenty of women. And the only cause you were worried about was your own. Logan's idea was actually—"

"Totally self-serving," Cameron retorted.

While the brothers debated the merit of Logan's fundraising abilities, I ambled over to the desk. Picking up the flyer, I scanned the list of charities, my eyes flickering over the seal for the American Diabetes Association.

I nudged the chair to get Chase's attention. "Does the charity have to be on this list?"

"No. Those are just a few of the more reputable organizations." He laced his fingers behind his head, appraising me. "Why? You got something better in mind?"

"I might." I folded the flyer and then tucked it away in my back pocket. "How long did you say we have to decide?

"A couple days, give or take."

"I'll let you know." Grabbing my backpack, I headed for the door. "Don't commit to anything before I get back to you."

In the parking lot, I slid behind the wheel of my truck and then pulled out my phone. I scrolled through the list of contacts from

Mel's study group, frowning when I came upon the name I was looking for.

My finger hovered over the text icon, but instead, I swallowed my pride and placed the call.

"Mitchell, this is Christian." Without waiting for a reply, I added, "Don't hang up. I need to talk to you about a fundraising event."

Standing in the shadows in the back of the Erwin Center, I waited for an hour while graduates walked the stage to collect their diplomas.

When the dean got to the "S's," I made my way down the outer aisle, heading for the tiny figure in the wheelchair two rows from the front.

As each name echoed in the auditorium, a chorus of cheers resounded from the audience. My heart sank when I knelt beside Mel's nana and saw the look of anticipation in her eyes, knowing she couldn't voice her pride.

"Mo." I tapped her shoulder. "It's Christian, Melody's friend." I maneuvered in front of her, careful not to block the stage. Though her face bore no emotion, the smile in her eyes warmed my insides. "Look, I just wanted to—"

The woman seated to Mo's right leaned forward, her features cloaked under the dim lights. "Can I help you?"

"I'm a friend of Melody's." I took a small blue box from the pocket of my jacket. "I'm just here to drop off a gift. It's actually from Mo. I picked it out, though."

"And you are?" Curiosity piqued the woman's tone.

"Christian." I smiled tightly at the couple in front of us who'd twisted in their seat to offer me an admonishing glare. "I'm not staying."

I gave the caregiver a polite nod before placing the tiny box on the blanket covering Mo's lap. "Give this to Mel for me, will you?"

Mo's green eyes locked on mine, and she blinked twice. I patted her hand as I stood.

My feet grew roots when I caught sight of Mel on the stage in her cap and gown.

I thought of holding my ground, standing proud so she'd know I was there.

Instead, I shrank against the wall and held my breath. Hearing her name, I let out a whoop and clapped loud enough to drown out the smattering of perfunctory applause from the strangers.

Mel took her diploma, her gaze flitting over the crowd.

I'm here, angel.

She didn't notice me lurking, but the brilliant smile that lit her face when she found her nana was worth the price of admission, even though I could feel my chest constricting with every breath. It was like she was stealing my air; tucking it away with everything else she took when she left.

Still, I paused for a moment to watch Melody glide down the steps. When she took her seat, I lost her in the sea of burnt orange caps. So I turned on my heel and powered toward the exit, chased away by the scent of autumn that was sure to engulf me if I waited a second longer.

Chapter 16

The crowd at The Parish roared so loud I didn't hear Logan's footsteps until he patted me on the back.

"They're turning people away at the door." He peeked around the curtain. "I think if we pack one more body in this place the fire marshal will shut us down."

"It's a great turnout," I agreed. "Any idea how much money we raised?"

"Nope." He shrugged. "But Chase offered to match the amount, and he's throwing in all the liquor sales to boot."

Sean sauntered up, twirling his timeworn drumsticks with Cameron at his heels.

"Leave it to you to wear a ribbon instead of a bracelet," Sean joked, flicking the green and blue satin strip pinned to my T-shirt. "Next time, you should tie it in your hair."

The guys proudly sported the "Cure PSP" plastic bracelets that we were giving out at the door.

But not me. The skin on my wrist was too raw from my freshly minted tattoo.

Picking up my bass, I slipped the strap over my shoulder. "What can I say? I'm a trendsetter."

Shifting from foot to foot, adrenaline surged through my veins as we waited for our cue.

When the house lights dimmed, Logan held the curtain open, tipping his chin to the stage.

"Why don't you make the announcement? This is your event, bro."

Front and center was Logan's stock and trade. He rarely gave up a chance to bask in the glory of our fans, even for a second.

With a small nod, I mumbled my thanks and then strode toward the blinding spotlight. The crowd let out an earsplitting cheer as I took the mic.

"How y'all doing tonight? I'm Christian." Smiling, I paused as another round of applause shook the rafters. "Thanks for coming out to our fundraiser for Cure PSP. All the proceeds for tonight's show are earmarked for a research grant to take place right here at UT." The weight on my shoulders lifted a little at the enthusiastic response. "Here's to fighting the good fight! Let's get this party started!"

The ground shook as Logan joined me. Snaking an arm around my neck, he shouted into the mic, "Let's here it for Christian! He planned this shindig!"

Another loud roar threatened to blow the roof off the place. I held up a hand, nodding my thanks before retreating to my usual spot next to Cameron.

"You done good, man," he yelled.

Plastering on a fake smile, I nodded, waiting for the show to start. Moments later, with the party clamoring around me, I closed my eyes and willed the music to carry me away. But the magic wasn't there.

My logic failed me and now I was paying the price. Daily.

Feelings didn't fade with time, as I'd always believed. Two days into winter—hell, only two more days until Christmas—and I wasn't close to being over Mel.

With every breath I took, at the edge of every thought, she was there. And as long as she stayed, time held no meaning.

No matter what the calendar said, my love for the girl that smelled like a season trapped me in fall.

Chapter 17

The Christmas tree in the corner of my living room mocked my misery as I weaved my way to the kitchen to grab another cup of coffee. Boxes and bags full of ornaments, lights, and tinsel, sat unused in the corner of the room where they'd been since I hauled the decorations from the attic.

Sighing, I poured the last of the bitter brew into Mel's old UT mug, while lyrics cluttered my thoughts. I wasn't the writer in the group—that was Cameron—but I'd been known to contribute a song here and there. And I'd been stuck on this one for days.

Dropping onto the couch, I flipped open the leather bound journal and reread some of the lyrics.

Lost in Fall . . .

Autumn's gone, baby, but you still remain. Under my skin, tumbling 'round my brain.

Leaves have fallen, and the writing's on the wall. You're not coming back, but I'm lost in fall.

My phone buzzed, pulling me from my thoughts. Blowing out a breath, I read the text from Logan.

Where are you? Lily won't let us open presents until you get here.

My gaze shifted to the single gift under my bare tree. The only one I'd bothered to wrap.

Raking a hand through my unkempt hair, I pondered for a minute before responding: *Y'all go ahead. I'm not feeling it. I might swing by later.*

The phone beeped with Logan's reply before I could set it down.

Get your ass up, take a shower, and get over here. Or we're coming to you.

The screen darkened while I weighed my options. Glancing out the picture window, I noted the droplets of rain and gray skies. Central Texas offered no white Christmases to speak of, but winter made her presence known.

Shaking off the gloom, I tossed the phone on the table as I headed for the stairs. Logan was a man of his word: if I didn't get my head out of my ass and join in the celebration, they'd bring the celebration to me. And that's the last thing I wanted.

I stood under the steady stream of pulsing water in the shower longer than I intended, but the warmth helped thaw some of the chill that had settled in my bones.

As I stepped into my pants, the doorbell echoed in the foyer.

Fuck.

"Coming!" I took the stairs two at a time, tugging a T-shirt over my head.

Raking a hand through my damp hair, I plastered on a smile and opened the door. "You guys really didn't . . ." The words died on my lips when I met the most beautiful green eyes I'd ever seen.

"Melody," I croaked. "What are you doing here?"

Clutching a brightly wrapped package to her chest, her exposed skin glistened from the droplets of rain.

"I'm sorry for dropping by without calling." She held out the present with shaking hands. "I wanted to give you this. And thank you for hosting the fundraiser at The P-Parish."

Her mouth curved into a smile despite her chattering teeth.

"You're freezing." I wedged the package under my arm and then pulled her into the house. "Why aren't you wearing a coat?"

She crossed her arms over her rain-soaked shirt. "It wasn't supposed to storm today. I checked the forecast and everything."

Her bottom lip jutted out as she shook, fighting off the chills trembling her body.

Placing a hand on her back, electricity shot up my arm. "Let's get you warmed up."

She tucked a wet strand of hair behind her ear. "It's okay. I don't want to disturb you."

Disturb me. Please disturb me. Talk to me. Yell at me. Just don't leave.

"You're not disturbing me." Unfurling my fingers when I noticed I was fisting the back of her shirt, I motioned toward the living room.

"Let me put a log on the fire. We can talk."

Snagging her lip between her teeth, she nodded. "If you're sure."

I wasn't sure of much anymore, but I knew one thing: if Mel tried to leave she'd have to get past me to do it.

"I'm sure."

Mel's soggy sneakers left puddles of water in their wake as I guided her toward the living room.

She sank onto the sofa and smiled, grazing the thick brocade with her fingertips. Recalling all the times we made love in that very spot, I smiled too.

She shivered, catapulting my thoughts back to the present. Snatching the blanket from the corner of the couch, I slipped the soft velour over her shoulders.

My hands lingered a moment too long and she looked up at me. "Christian . . ."

Hearing the admonishment in her tone, I took a step back.

"Let me get that fire started." I wiped my sweaty palms on my jeans as I strolled to the hearth. "I've got some of that special hot chocolate you like."

Mel's eyes widened and her smile grew. "Stephen's?"

"Yeah, I picked some up at Whole Foods," I admitted. "I've got some diab—sugar-free cookies too."

"Why?" Curiosity piqued her tone. "You're not a diabetic."

The word rolled off her tongue with an ease I'd never heard.

"Someone once told me that sugar kills." Breaking our gaze, I returned to my preparations. "She was pretty smart, so I took her advice."

Truth be told, I'd replaced all the items in my pantry with their sugar-free counterparts.

Even as I'd done it, I knew it was insane. There was no reason to believe Mel would return. No equation that put my odds above a fraction of a percent.

Yet, here she was, sitting on my couch.

Tossing a log on the dying embers from this morning's fire, sparks flew in every direction.

"I'll have this going in a second," I assured her. "You'll be warm in no time."

When I got no acknowledgement, I turned to find Melody staring down at the leather-bound notebook.

"I didn't know you wrote poetry." Smiling softly, her fingertips glided over the lyrics.

"I don't." Stoking the fire, the resultant heat warmed my already burning cheeks. "That's going to be a song when it grows up." Brushing off my hands, I wobbled to my feet. "So—hot chocolate? Coffee? Tea?"

"It sounds like poetry." She closed the journal, smiling. "The hot chocolate would be great, if it's not too much trouble."

Running a hand through her hair, tiny beads of rain fell from the soaked tendrils, disappearing into the valley between her breasts.

"I've got some clean T-shirts in the . . . um . . ." I hit the wall as I backed away. "Let me just get you one."

Cursing at my inability to hold my shit together, I stomped to the laundry room and rooted around the basket of clean laundry.

Be cool.

Cool went right out the window when I returned and found Mel seated in front of the fireplace, the velour blanket draped loosely over her bare shoulders.

Gazing at the fire with her damp hair in a messy bun on the top of her head, she looked like the angel I'd always proclaimed her to be.

As I approached, I could just make out the numbers on her tattoo.

"Here you go." I handed her the dry garment, then knelt beside her to stoke the fire.

After Mel finished dressing, she rubbed her hands together and held them closer to the flames.

"I wanted to thank you for hosting the fundraiser," she said quietly. "I had no idea. I mean . . . I would have helped. But you didn't call, so . . ."

I set down the poker in the rack and then turned to face her.

Easing a damp strand of hair from her eyes, I twirled the length around my finger.

"You broke up with me," I reminded her. "I didn't want you to think I was using the event to get you to talk to me."

"I didn't breakup with you. I let you off the hook. You seemed relieved at the time."

At the time, I knew no better. Hell, I still didn't know much, except that I wanted her in every way.

"You didn't give me much choice."

Before I could rewind and explain myself, Mel was on her feet, glaring down at me.

"And what was I supposed to do? I was already in love with you. We didn't fit. We still don't fit." Eyes wide, her hand flew to her mouth. "I have to go."

With all she said, only three words stood out. She loved me.

I grabbed her hand before she could bolt.

"Please don't go, Mel. I was wrong about so many things. I know I didn't put up much of a fight. But you have to believe—"

She shook her head. "I tried, Christian. I really did. But I don't belong in your world. I can't stay up all night and I can't—"

"Angel, listen to me. I partied and went to clubs for years. But I don't miss it. I'd rather spend time with you, in any world that you're in. But as I remember, you had a pretty good time at The Parish until I dragged you out of the place."

"That wasn't your fault. I overdid it." She frowned. "I was trying to prove a point—maybe to myself. I don't know."

Her shoulders sank, her brows drawing together at the recollection.

"I was worried about you that night. You're an adult. You can do what you want. But..." Tightening my grip, I held on tight as I passed the point of no return. "I love you. And I don't want anything to happen to you. You can't ask me not to love you, angel. I've tried."

Mel sank down next to me, stunned. "I thought you didn't believe in love."

"I didn't, until I met you."

The faint silver rimming her pupils sparkled in the reflected light from the fire. Entwining our fingers, she shifted her gaze to the roaring inferno and didn't say a word. Since she was still here, I was fine with that.

"Do you still want some hot chocolate?"

Shaking her head, she looked down at our joined hands. Her brow creased as she brushed her index finger along the inside of my wrist, tracing the tattoo that matched her own.

"Euler's Identity . . ." Her eyes darted to mine. "Why?"

Calculating the odds, I thought her too stunned to put up much of a fight, so I pulled her onto my lap. My chest expanded as I took my first unhindered breath since she walked out the door.

"You'd have to ask Euler. He thought it up. I got it because it reminds me of you. The perfect equation," I kissed her nose, "for the perfect woman."

She grimaced. "I'm not perfect. I'm—"

"Of course you're not perfect. You're a smartass with a huge ego. But I can live with that." I eased her onto her back. "As long as I have you."

She circled my wrist, brushing her thumb over the tattoo once again. "It still adds up to zero. It'll always be zero."

"Zero isn't the end, angel. It's the beginning. Everything starts with zero."

Brushing my lips over the corner of her mouth, I waited for the protest that was certain to follow.

"But . . ."

I silenced her with a passionate kiss, drowning in her sweet scent. I'd grown to believe she was my air. The fact I couldn't breathe without her proved the hypothesis. When my lungs threatened to burst, I had to pull away, so some oxygen was obviously necessary.

Resting my forehead against hers, I gathered my reserves so I could make another go at her mouth. "You're lost in fall."

"Lost in fall?" she panted, her breathing as ragged as mine.

My hand crept under her baggy T-shirt. "You smell like autumn. But I thought you might change with the season. Like maybe that was your superpower."

"That would be a lame superpower," she mused. "But then again, I'm a girl who's brought to her knees by gummy bears."

I frowned. "Don't say that, Melody. You're the strongest person I've ever met."

She held out her arm, examining the Tiffany bracelet I'd given her for graduation.

"'She believed she could, so she did,'" Mel whispered, reciting the phrase that was stamped on the inside of the platinum cuff.

"Yep. But I know something besides gummy bears that can bring you to your knees." I nipped her bottom lip. "Metaphorically speaking."

Laughter erupted from her chest. "Missed having me on my knees, did you?"

Popping the button on her jeans, I fingered the little bow on her panties. "You have no idea."

Her brows turned inward as she looked into my eyes. "Have you been, um, seeing anyone...you know, since I've been gone?"

I blinked down at her, too stunned to answer.

"It's all right if you have," she was quick to reply. "It's not like we were together or anything."

"Does my hand count?" I tried for a somber expression. "Because we've had quite a few dates." Laughter threatened, unfamiliar, since I hadn't felt it in weeks. "You two are already acquainted so we can probably make it a threesome. Or would that be a foursome?"

When I could stand it no more, the chuckle broke free and I fell onto my back, pulling her down with me.

Since the joke was at her expense, she scampered on top of me and poked my chest, a mock pout jutting her lip. "Very funny."

I pulled the knot at the top of her head, setting her blond locks free. All traces of humor left me as I slid my hand into the damp strands.

"I could barely breathe without you, angel. I love you so much. I couldn't—"

She pressed her lips to mine. Gently. And only for a second. "I love you too. I just don't know how this is going to go."

When I guided her mouth to mine for another kiss, I knew that the invisible fingers encasing my heart were real. Because I felt them ease the minute I tasted her cherry lip balm.

Reversing our position, I repeated the words I told her the first night we were together. "It goes how it goes. I love you. And I want you. I don't care what the odds are, I'll take them."

"It goes how it goes," she repeated. "That's pretty rational, in an irrational sort of way."

Before she started thinking too much, which always got her into trouble, I claimed her mouth. The need inside me grew with every twist of her tongue, but I wanted to savor her. Once I lost myself inside her, it would be over quick.

Impatient as ever, it didn't take very long before she was clawing at my T-shirt.

I rose to my knees, not surprised that her pants were unzipped.

"All right, angel. Let's get you out of these clothes."

She stretched like a cat, then lay surprisingly still while I undressed her. Her hand snaked to her belly when I was finished.

"Don't even think about it," I warned, as I stripped out of my clothes. "Any sudden moves, and I'm tying you to a chair."

Biting her lip, her fingers inched lower. I guess threatening my girl with a good time wasn't going to work.

I was about to slide out of my boxers when I realized I didn't have a condom.

Reluctantly, I headed for the stairs.

"No touching." I shot her a warning look over my shoulder. "I'll be right back."

When I returned her gaze dropped to the foil packet in my hand.

She propped on her elbow. "Are you . . . I mean . . . have you been tested?"

I dropped to my knees, ripping the package open with my teeth. "Routinely."

I was about to roll the latex into place when I noted her troubled expression.

She managed to give me a small, unenthused smile. "That's reassuring, I guess."

Abandoning the condom for the moment, I crawled up until we were nose to nose.

"I've never had unsafe sex. The reason I've been tested has more to do with the insurance riders from the promoters and the record label."

Relaxing, she ran a lazy finger over my jaw. "I have an IUD. It's safer that way. Someone like me, with my diabetes, I can't risk an unplanned pregnancy. But if you're sure, we don't have to use anything."

I was sure. Ninety-nine-point-nine percent. That one-tenth of a percent kept me from taking her up on the offer.

"I'll take another test. But right now, I just want to love you."

I took another moment, memorizing every freckle on her face. She came to me every night in my dreams, but this was so much better.

I kissed a path to her perfect breasts, sucking one rose tipped peak into my mouth. When she started squirming, I rocked back on my heels.

Sliding the latex over my shaft, I smiled at the thought of being inside her with nothing between us. But even I couldn't get my doctor to make a house call on Christmas Day.

"Christian?"

Grinning at her impatience, I wrapped her legs around my waist.

Guiding myself to her entrance, I slid in an inch, then worked her tiny nub with patience until her fists began to clench.

"You like that?"

She nodded, and I slipped all the way in. Home. I was finally home.

My thumb continued to thrum her swollen clit while I moved inside her. When her eyes fluttered closed, I eased myself on top of her, rolling my hips with each thrust.

Her brows scrunched in that way they always did when she was searching for something just beyond her reach. "Christian . . . oh, God . . . I . . ."

She increased the pace, her fingers digging into my shoulders.

I brushed a kiss to her mouth when I felt her shatter, and then followed her into the abyss.

"That's it, angel," I whispered. "Fall with me."

Chapter 18

I brushed Mel's foot under the dining room table. "You okay?" I mouthed.

She nodded, giving me a small smile as she picked at her food, her eyes darting to the horde of people that had descended on the house.

When I answered Logan's call and told him I'd be spending Christmas at my place with Mel, they brought the party to us. That worked for me, but my girl looked just this side of overwhelmed.

Chase sat at the other end of the table, quiet as usual. His scruffy beard, grown out for the winter, made him look more like the musician he was, than the businessman that everyone assumed he to be. In truth, he was both.

He gave me an easy smile, patting me on the back as he left the room to take a call.

Lily sidestepped Chase on her way out of the kitchen, a pie balanced on each of her palms. "How's your nana, Mel?"

Mel swallowed hard and reached for her water, her eyes meeting mine over the rim of the glass. "She's fine. I saw her this morning."

"Let me know if you ever want company." Lily slid the pies onto the table. "When you visit her, I mean."

Mel cleared her throat. "I . . . um . . . that's very nice of you. She doesn't speak, though. She knows everything that's going on around her, but she has trouble getting the words out."

"That's all right," Cameron interjected, fighting Logan for the dessert dish. "Lily's great with people. And once you get her going, she talks enough for everyone."

"I do not." Lily pried the pie plate out of the guys' hands and then cut the dessert into equal slices. "I went to the CurePSP website. I know she can't speak. But that doesn't mean she wouldn't enjoy some visitors."

"She would, very much," Mel said softly. "Thank you."

Logan finished the last bite of his pie and then pushed to his feet. "Its time for presents," he announced. "I've been waiting all fucking day for presents. I'm going to start unwrapping shit if y'all don't get a move on."

Mel picked up a couple of plates while everyone followed Logan to the living room.

Taking the dishes from her hands, I set them on the table. "Leave those. I've got to go keep an eye on things, or Logan's liable to open everyone's shit." I pressed a kiss to her lips. "Even yours."

Before Mel could protest, I pulled her towards the ruckus in the other room.

Sinking into the leather chair, I gathered her onto my lap. "Y'all's gifts are in bags in the closet. I didn't wrap anything yet."

Logan shot me a glare as he handed a package to Lily. "Where's your Christmas spirit, asshat?"

I smiled. "My Christmas spirit didn't show up until a few hours ago." I jiggled my knee, and Mel settled against my chest.

Logan read the tag on the silver package that was tucked behind the tree. "This one says 'Melody.'" He grinned. "But it doesn't say who it's from. So I'll just take credit for it." He dropped the gift in her arms. "Enjoy, sweetheart."

Mel ran her hand over the metallic paper before lifting her gaze to me. "I'm assuming this is from you?"

I shrugged. "Better open it to make sure."

Scooting off my lap, she picked up the present she'd brought with her, holding the package out for me to take. "You first."

"We'll open them together."

Satisfied, she returned to my lap and tore open her gift while I fiddled with the paper on mine. Her brow creased when she opened up the folder. As she read the description, her chin trembled. "Christian . . ."

I caught the tear that spilled onto her cheek. "You know, it's probably just bullshit," I joked, carefully taking the certificate for the star I'd purchased in her nana's name. The bold letters described the exact coordinates where the Marina Sullivan star was located in the Pegasus Constellation. "But I'll take you both to the planetarium to check it out anyway."

"Thank you," she croaked, placing the certificate back in the leather folder. "I love it." She ran her hands over the cover and then looked up at me. "I love you."

"I love you too." I kissed her nose. "But I think there's something else in the box."

Smiling, I peeled back the heavy wrapping on my package, revealing a thick blue book. I swallowed hard as I opened the cover of the first edition copy of *Relativity* by Albert Einstein.

"Mel . . . this is . . ."

"Do you like it?" She clutched the small cloth bag she'd retrieved from her box, still unaware of the contents.

"I love it." I cleared my throat. "But you shouldn't have. This is a first edition."

She shrugged. "I recently got my first job on this research project my boyfriend held a fundraiser for." She grinned. "I'm rolling in dough."

I knew for a fact that Mel's salary was minimal. And I also knew how much the book cost. I was still gazing at the cover when she let out a gasp.

"Oh my God," she breathed, lifting the two-carat, star-shaped diamond pendant from the velvet box I'd stowed inside the bag. "I . . . oh . . ." She looked up at me, eyes wide. "It's beautiful."

Any guy that tells you that chicks don't like diamonds is lying to your face. At least, if my girl was any indication.

"It's got the coordinates of your nana's star lasered into the stone," I whispered as I fastened the clasp around her neck. "So she'll always be with you."

Mel buried her face in my neck, her shoulders quaking as she let out a quiet sob. "Thank you."

"Somebody's been really good," Logan crowed. "Or really bad. What did you get her, Wikipedia?"

"'Wikipedia'?" Swiping at the tears, Mel's curiosity got the better of her, and she turned to the group. "Why do you call him 'Wikipedia'?"

"He's a geek." Logan wrinkled his nose. "Look at him."

Scrunching her brow, she examined my tattooed arms and day old scruff before swinging her gaze back to Logan. "Um, no, he's *not*. I'm a geek. So I would know."

Logan smirked, taking a sip of his beer. "No, sweetie, you're hot." He pointed at me. "But he's a geek. Or a nerd." He scratched his head. "Or a geek-nerd."

Mel crossed her arms over her chest, narrowing her eyes at the guy who was more like a brother to me than a friend. "He's not a geek, or a nerd. Or a geek-nerd." Reclining against my chest with that sexy-as-hell defiant look on her face, she fingered the pendant around her neck. "He's perfect."

Money well spent.

I discreetly shot Logan the finger.

He scowled, shifting a wary gaze to Mel.

Since he looked more intimidated by her than me, I dropped a kiss to the top of her head for good measure. "You tell him, angel."

"You'd better keep a hold of that one," Cameron interjected with a chuckle. "She obviously suffers from the same disease my girl has." He smiled down at Lily, tucked against his side. "Blind as a bat or some kind of brain damage."

Mel's autumn scent enveloped me as I tightened my grip on her waist. "Oh, I'm holding on. For as long as she lets me."

The End . . .

EPILOGUE

One Year Later

I rolled over onto my side, and pulled the covers over my head to block out the Christmas music spilling into Christian's bedroom.

My bedroom.

That was going to take some getting used to. I'd moved in with Christian six months ago because it didn't make sense to keep paying for an apartment that I didn't live in.

My research grant was extended for another year—thanks to the endowment that Chase Noble had set up. The Phoenix Group was now the single largest supporter of PSP research in the state.

But none of it would help Nana.

I always knew it. But now that her illness had progressed, I had to face the fact that anything I'd done wouldn't make a difference. Not for her.

Christian was trying so hard to make this holiday one to remember. Because no matter what, it would be Nana's last. That thought alone had stolen all my joy, and I couldn't shake the depression.

The mattress dipped, and Christian burrowed under the covers with me, banding his arms around my waist. "Morning, angel." Feathering kisses over my shoulder, he worked his way to my ear. "Are you just going to hang out in here all day."

If only.

Christian's bandmates would never allow that to happen. Not that I was complaining. I'd spent years isolated, studying and taking care of Nana. Which didn't leave much time to make friends. But all that had changed after Christian and I got together.

Lily and I had a standing date once a week when the band was playing, and a mani-pedi appointment every Saturday. I'd never had a best friend, not since I was a kid, and she was that for me. But with the holidays, and Nana's rapid deterioration, I'd begged off the last two weeks in a row.

I turned over and, pressing my forehead to Christian's shoulder, I released a tremulous breath. "I have to go visit Nana." Tears pricked the back of my eyes. "And I don't know what kind of company I'll be after that. Maybe you should plan on doing the Christmas Eve thing alone."

"Angel..." My heart squeezed, hearing the disappointment in his voice. "Look at me."

Sniffling, I wiped away a stray tear and then lifted my gaze.

Christian smiled that soft smile, and said, "I knew you'd say that, so I decided to have Christmas Eve here."

My stomach dropped, and I frowned, shaking my head. "Christian... No..."

His hands slid to my ass. "This isn't healthy, Mel. You can't lock yourself up in this room and wait for the bottom to fall out. Let me be here for you."

I wanted nothing more than to let Christian share this burden, but it was too much. "You should've told me before you invited everyone over."

He stroked my back with gentle fingers. "So you could stress about it all week?"

It was maddening how well this man knew me.

Christian took my sigh as a sign of capitulation and he rolled me onto my back. I felt so safe under the covers with him, that I couldn't even be mad.

Slipping his hand under my nightshirt, he palmed my breast. "I love you, angel."

He captured my mouth, sliding his tongue between my parted lips. My body reacted, and my mind followed, and suddenly there was nothing but him.

He got up and began to undress while I watched.

"No you don't," he said, catching my wrist when my hand dipped into my panties. "When are you going to learn some patience?"

Never.

I feared it was the truth. I'm sure most women could look at Christian, and that would be enough to send them into orbit. But not me.

The feelings were always there, the tightness in my belly and the tingle between my legs, but my body refused to cooperate more often than not.

Easing on top of me, he pushed my nightshirt under my arms. I gasped when he sucked my nipple into his mouth. "Relax, baby."

Christian knew what I needed. What I craved.

My fingers twined into his hair as he moved lower. When he reached the juncture of my thighs, he rasped, "Open for me."

My overstimulated mind began to race, and I dug my heels into the mattress.

"Easy," he whispered, skimming his palm over my calf. "I've got you."

And then his fingers were inside me, curled in that way that insured that he *did* have me. That he owned me.

I groaned again as his tongue slid between my folds.

"Don't stop...please..."

He chuckled, because after a year and some months he'd never stopped. Not until I was a quivering mess and completely sated.

His tongue began the familiar dance against my swollen clit, and I rolled my hips to find the elusive rhythm.

"Be still, angel. Let it happen."

I nodded, following his order, and within a moment the pleasure ripped through me and I shattered into a million pieces.

"Fuck...fuck...*yes*..."

While I tried to recover, he eased on top of me, smiling wickedly. "Told you."

My retort died on a moan when Christian buried himself in one thrust. Circling his hips, he put pressure on my already sensitive nub.

"Come for me," he bit out. "Let me feel you."

And though I wouldn't have thought it was possible before we met, I did just that. As I spiraled to the bottom, Christian picked up the pace, exploding inside me as I clenched around him.

I envied him that, the control he had over his body. He could make it last for a half hour, or reach the finish line in a few good thrusts.

He rested his forehead against mine, grinning. "Merry Christmas, angel."

A few hours later, when I heard people milling around downstairs, I reluctantly hauled myself out of bed. I still had to visit Nana, which would give me an excuse to slip out of the house so I wouldn't ruin the holiday for everyone else.

As I descended the staircase, I froze when I spotted Christian, crouched beside the recliner. He assessed me with soft eyes. "Come down here, angel. Someone wants to see you."

The room fell silent and everyone swung their gazes in my direction.

"Ah, for fuck sake," Logan grumbled as he pushed off the sofa. "Get down here." Grabbing my hand, he dragged me toward my boyfriend. "We can't start this little shindig without you."

My attention snapped to the big leather chair where Nana sat, eyes locked on mine, and fingers working furiously on the hem of her festive red sweater.

"Nana." I croaked as I rushed to kneel in front of her.

Christian leaned close to my ear and said, "Mo decided she was tired of living at the home. So I thought maybe she could stay with us awhile." He smiled at Nana. "Until she gets a place of her own, of course."

A lump the size of a baseball formed in my throat when Nana blinked twice. I forced a smile, even as my heart broke. "I...I'll be right back..."

Staggering to my feet, I rushed to the kitchen with Christian on my heels.

"What is it?" he asked, grabbing my arm to stop my fidgeting. "I thought you wanted Nana at home. I heard you talking to the doctor about the logistics of moving her in with you."

"Of course I want her with me," I cried. "But she needs twenty-four-hour care and I...I can't..."

He folded me into his arms. "Nobody can take care of Mo by themselves. I wasn't suggesting that. I've got three nurses on standby. Two for the day shift, and one that will be here at night. A live-in."

Shaking my head, I looked down at my toes. "Christian, you've never seen Nana agitated. She screams. Sometimes for an hour. She gets so frustrated."

Cupping my cheek, he gently brought my gaze to his. "Does that bother you?"

My mouth dropped open. "No...of course not. It's not me that I'm worried about."

He chuckled, then pressed a kiss to my lips. "I play rock music for a living...with Logan Cage. If he's not wailing onstage, he's bitching about something or another." I hiccuped a laugh, and Christian turned serious. "Mo doesn't have...She doesn't have a lot of time, baby."

Hearing Christian say it, made it real. Inevitable. The sob I'd so valiantly tried to stifle broke free. "You'd do that for me? For Nana?"

Christian's hands sank into my hair, and he anchored his forehead to mine. "I'd do anything for you."

I squeezed my eyes shut. "But this is your home. I was trying to figure out how to... I don't know, move us into a place for a few months until..."

She died. I couldn't even say it.

Christian pulled me flush against his chest. "This is *our* home. Let me do this for you."

His heartbeat steady beneath my touch. He wanted to do this.

For me.

I nodded, so full of love, I could barely speak. "Thank you."

I sank onto my haunches beside Nana, holding her hand as Christian passed out presents. I must've been the only one who wasn't in on this plan because soon there was a mountain of gifts stacked up beside her chair. I put a small present on her lap and then watched as she tore it open.

After the rest of the gifts were unwrapped, Christian took a seat on the floor next to me. "That was hard work," he complained. "Get me a beer, angel?"

Reflexively, my brow arched. But then he gave me puppy dog eyes, and I hauled to my feet. How could I not? The man had just given me the best present ever. *Time.*

When I returned, my steps faltered when I found him on one knee beside Nana's chair.

"Come here, angel." I swallowed hard as I closed the gap between us. He took my hand. "Mo and I were talking. She's got a problem with us living in sin." He grinned as he took out a box from his pocket. "I mean, I'm fine with it, but since Mo is going to be living here, you know, we might as well make her happy."

I didn't have the heart to tell Christian that Nana didn't marry granddaddy until five years after my mom was born. And that was only because they didn't want their daughter to enter kindergarten with unwed parents.

I gasped when he popped the lid on the small wooden box, revealing a beautiful—and extremely large—oval diamond. Christian's smile faded. "Will you marry me, Melody?"

My attention turned to Nana, rocking excitedly in the chair. She blinked twice when our eyes met.

Sinking to my knees, I threw my arms around Christian's neck. "Yes."

He placed the stone on my trembling finger, and everyone clapped.

"I love you, angel," he murmured.

Burying my face in the crook of his neck, I cried softly. Tears of joy. And promise. And love.

And forever.

THE REAL MARINA SULLIVAN

This book wouldn't be complete if I didn't tell you a little about the inspiration for the character of Melody's nana, Marina "Mo" Sullivan.

Inspiration isn't a strong enough word.

Mo was a real person. She was my nana—the woman who raised me.

Like Mo, Nana loved to dance and sing. She spoke three languages and had the most beautiful green eyes I'd ever seen. She also had Progressive Supranuclear Palsy. PSP.

Two years before Nana passed, I made her a scrapbook. The cover was blue and purple and embossed with butterflies.

Since the project was an emotional undertaking, it took me months to gather all the photos and write the captions that wove together the tapestry of my nana's life. By the time I presented her with the gift on Christmas Day 2004, she was confined to a wheel-chair and largely nonverbal. I thought maybe I was too late. That she'd slipped beyond the point of comprehension.

But like always, Nana still had a few lessons to teach me—most notably on the resilience of the human spirit. Because not only did she understand, she sat with the little book of memories on her lap for hours. For days after that, she insisted on pouring over the pictures and small mementos that graced the pages so often the hinges finally came off the cover.

Months later, when Nana's condition had deteriorated further, I put the book away.

Fast-forward to December 23, 2006.

As our family was preparing for our Christmas celebration, Nana stopped eating. Just stopped. For two days, I refused to see the truth... that she was slipping away. But on December 25th, as I watched Nana sitting in her favorite chair in front of the fire, it dawned on me that no matter what, this would be her last Christmas.

So, like Melody, I frantically dug out the scrapbook from a box in my closet. And when I lay the book on Nana's lap, she cried silent tears as I turned the pages one last time.

Less than twenty-four hours later, she slipped into a coma. And for the next six nights, my daughter and I took turns sleeping on the floor next to her bed.

In the early hours of January 2, 2006, I went upstairs to take a shower. I don't know why since it was the middle of the night. But I've come to believe it was Nana—protecting me, like always. Because in those few moments I was gone, she found her wings.

As I mentioned in the book, people who suffer from PSP have no control over their features. There are no smiles or frowns.

But when I slipped back into the room, the first thing I noticed was the slight upturn of her lips. It was her parting gift, and more precious than anything she'd ever given me. It was goodbye.

So, while there is no Marina Sullivan, her spirit lives in the pages of my little book.

In case you're wondering, her real name was Augustina Geraldine.

But she hated that name. Everyone just called her Jeri.

For more information on Progressive Supranuclear Palsy visit: CUREPSP.ORG

PREVIEW

Missing From Me—Sixth Street Bands # 3

Chapter One
4 YEARS AGO
Sean

The front door slammed, shaking the walls in our small apartment. I snuggled closer to Anna's side and buried my face in her hair.

Logan's agitated voice cut through the fog of near sleep.

"Dude, wake up!"

Whatever mess my best friend had gotten himself into, he'd have to solve it on his own. This was one of Anna's rare mornings off, and since we'd had the apartment to ourselves, we'd stayed up late, listening to the rain and having lazy sex until we'd passed out.

Smiling at the thought of a repeat, I grumbled in Logan's general direction, "Go away. I don't have any condoms. Carry your ass to the store like a normal person and leave us alone."

His footsteps echoed in the tiny room, and then he was beside me, his long fingers digging into my shoulder as he gave me a hard shake. "I'm serious. Get up."

Not happening.

A frustrated groan escaped my lips when Anna twisted in my arms. She propped herself up on one elbow, wiping the sleep from her eyes. "What do you need, Lo?"

A swift kick in the ass.

Rolling onto my back, I smothered my face with the pillow, hoping he'd get the hint. Of course, he didn't.

Cursing under his breath, Logan rooted around under the comforter.

"Hey!" I snarled, tossing the pillow at him. "Whatever you're looking for, I don't have it."

Running an agitated hand through his blond hair, Logan glared at me.

"Where's your remote?" Anxiety laced his tone when I didn't answer right away. "For the TV, douchebag—where's the remote?"

Anna fumbled around on the nightstand and then handed him the clunky device. "What's wrong with the TV in your room?"

Logan walked to the end of the bed and took a seat.

Anna sat up, scowling. "Make it quick." She slumped against the headboard, glaring at the back of Logan's head. "Seriously, Lo, hurry up. I have to pee."

Logan ignored her, all his attention focused on the screen as he flipped through the channels. His shoulders sagged when he reached CNN.

Cable News? Now he had my attention. The only things Logan ever watched were MTV, VH1, or the Cartoon Network.

I popped up to see what was so important, but something told me I didn't want to know. "What's going on?"

"Quiet," Logan whispered.

Buttoning my lip, I reluctantly focused on the screen where a stone-faced commentator stood in a field, fat droplets of rain pelting her microphone.

"...live footage from the scene of the tragic accident outside of Freder-

icksburg, Texas this morning where two members of the super-group Damaged lost their lives in a fiery crash. At this point, we're unable to confirm the identities of the deceased. Damaged, arguably the hottest band in the country, just completed a series of shows in the Southwest and..."

The camera panned out for a wide-angle shot. Wisps of smoke rose from the wreckage, dissolving into the gray morning sky.

A gasp from Anna. "Oh my God."

She crumbled against me, her small hand curving around my waist as she buried her face in my chest. Unable to make sense of what I was seeing, I stroked her hair with numb fingers.

After a few moments of stunned silence, Logan jumped to his feet. "What the fuck is she smiling about?"

Confused, I blinked at him. "Who?"

"The fucking reporter." He pointed at the TV with a shaky hand. "What the hell is she grinning for?"

I shifted my gaze back to the screen, and sure as shit, the reporter was smiling. Just a slight upturn of her glossy lips.

I tightened my grip on my girl. "It's her job, man. She doesn't..." Emotion clogged my throat, and I struggled for breath. For words. "She doesn't know them."

But then, neither did we. Not really. Damaged hailed from Austin, our hometown. And over the last five years, as their star ascended, our paths had crossed on occasion.

Our band, Caged, was one of the many groups on Sixth Street that loosely followed the Damaged blueprint. Since high school, we'd been playing the same bars where Damaged got their start, hoping a little of their magic would rub off.

The news report abruptly cut to KVUE, the local ABC affiliate. Terri Gruca, the nighttime anchor, sat stoically behind the half-lit desk, her co-anchor nowhere in sight.

"Thank you, Sandy." Terri blinked into the camera. "We've just got word at the studio that Rhenn Grayson, lead singer for the Grammy winning band Damaged, and Paige Dawson, lead guitarist, were pronounced dead at the scene of the accident on Highway 290 this morning." She looked down at the copy wobbling in her shaking hand. "Rhenn's wife, singer Tori Grayson, and drummer, Miles Cooper, were airlifted to Brackenridge Hospital via Care Flight. According to band manager, Taryn Ayers, Mrs. Grayson and Mr. Cooper are both in critical condition. The bus driver was also pronounced dead at the crash site." Still photos of Rhenn and Paige appeared on a split screen in the background behind Terri's head. "Our prayers go out to the families. After a brief commercial break, we'll cut to the CNN studio for further updates on this tragedy and a look back at the lives of these two gifted musicians."

My head pounded as a commercial for toaster strudel flickered across the screen. Smiling faces and cheery voices, touting the virtue of strawberry jam tucked inside a fluffy pastry shell. Somewhere, people were probably eating that shit.

But not Rhenn or Paige.

"They were twenty-four years old," Logan murmured.

As he turned to face me, questions clouded his arctic blue eyes. The same questions I'd seen every day since the first time we met. About death, and why it visited some while leaving others alone. Death was what brought Logan and me together, after all. Our shared bond. Two kids whose mothers would never sit at the long table in Mrs. Varner's classroom handing out cookies. Because our mothers had "passed."

That's the polite term people used when someone died. The same folks made sure to tell you they were "sorry for your loss."

Which I always found funny, since my mother wasn't lost. She was dead.

Rhenn's voice boomed from the speaker on the worn-out TV. Smiling his most iconic smile, he stood back to back with Paige as he crooned the band's latest hit.

I leaned forward to drink it all in. Because that's all that was left now, bits of light and shadow caught on tape.

Slithering from my loose hold, Anna stumbled to her feet. "I've got to pee."

Before she got away, I swung my legs over the side of the bed and then slipped my arms around her waist to pull her between my knees.

Resting my forehead against her chest, I breathed deeply, her peach scent soothing me like a balm. "I love you, Anna-baby."

She sifted her fingers through my hair until I stopped shaking, and then kissed the top of my head. "Love you too."

Reluctantly, I let her go, and she retreated into the tiny bathroom. Through the paper-thin walls, I heard her crying softly.

When she returned, her face splotchy and her eyes glistening with leftover tears, I gave her a soft smile and lifted the covers so she could crawl in beside me.

An hour later and we still hadn't moved, like if we stayed here, it wouldn't be real.

But it was.

When they showed the Care Flight helicopter on the roof of Brackenridge Hospital for the second time, I snapped. "Change that, will you?"

Logan flipped the channel to MTV while I reached for the pad of paper I kept beside the bed to jot down lyrics.

Like everyone else, the music channel was covering the Damaged story. But instead of reporting what everyone already knew, they were running a special broadcast about the three lesser-known bands that had followed Damaged up the ladder.

A solemn voice spoke over a montage of snippets flickering on the screen.

"While it stands to reason that Leveraged, Revenge Theory, or Drafthouse will fill the gaping hole left by today's tragic event, a few lesser-known groups from Austin have amassed quite a following."

Jolted by the familiar beat, my gaze snapped to the television where footage of Caged performing at the Parish flashed on the set.

"One such group, Caged, is currently playing the same venue where Damaged got their start some five years ago."

The camera panned to the front of my drum kit where the band's logo, a lion inside a gilded cage, shimmered under the lights.

"Like many of the smaller Sixth Street bands, Caged is still fighting for notoriety outside this small, but illustrious, stretch of road."

"Oh my God," Anna whispered, squeezing my hand. "That's you."

Guilt flooded my insides, sweeping away the momentary jubilation.

They're dead, I reminded myself, turning my attention back to my lyrics.

Voices dying on the breeze, eyes now see what no one sees.

Will you be among the masses, forever frozen as time passes?

As I pondered the morbid compilation, the incessant ringing roused me from my next thought.

"Answer that call, dude," I grumbled to Logan's back.

He glanced down at his hand as if he just realized he was holding the phone. Swiping a finger over the screen, he took a deep breath before lifting the device to his ear.

"Hey, Chase." Logan pushed to his feet and began to pace in a tight circle, glancing at the television every few seconds. "Of course I heard." Stopping in his tracks, he listened intently. "Tonight?" He glanced at me, brows drawn together over troubled blue eyes. "I don't know. Let me talk to Sean first."

Tossing the phone on the bed, Logan dropped his head back and stared at the ceiling. "That was Chase. He wants us to do a set tonight."

My stomach twisted as the shock rolled through me. "Why tonight?"

Logan's eyes met mine, conflicted. "There's going to be some kind of candlelight vigil." He cleared his throat. "They're expecting music, so someone's got to take the stage."

Might as well be us.

I could almost hear his unspoken thought.

"What do you think?" he asked, chewing the hell out of his thumbnail.

Looking past him at the screen, I watched as people gathered on Sixth Street. Some wandered aimlessly, tears streaming down their faces, while others stood reverently in front of the poster of Damaged that hung next to the entrance to the Parish. All of them needed one thing—closure.

Pushing aside my reservations, I shrugged. "Whatever. That's fine."

Logan nodded and then gazed at the screen one last time before wandering from the room.

When Anna followed, I assumed she was going to get something from the kitchen.

Burrowing into the pillow, I threw my arm over my eyes.

"Sean?"

Anna's whisper jerked me from my thoughts.

"Yeah?"

She gave me a watery smile as she stood by the door, twisting the hem of her nightshirt.

I offered her my hand. "Come here, baby."

She sank onto her heels at my side. Slashes of sunlight peeked through the slats in the worn mini blinds, turning her red hair into a fiery halo. She looked shocked to the core.

"I don't know what's wrong with me." A tear spilled onto her cheek. "It's not like I knew them or anything."

I wicked the moisture away with the pad of my thumb. "You didn't have to know them, baby. They meant something to you, and you're sad."

"I know." She sniffed, fiddling with her emerald ring. "But it's not like, you know, family." Our eyes met, and I could almost see the thought forming on her lips. "Not like your mom, or..."

I watched the column of her throat as she swallowed. The rise and fall of her chest. Anything to avoid the pity in her eyes.

Sliding a hand into her hair, I pulled her close. "That was a long time ago."

When her lips fell open to reply, I silenced her with a kiss. Cradling the back of her head, I reversed our positions. She moaned softly as I pulled her leg to my waist.

"Maybe we shouldn't."

Her breathy pant held no conviction, so I kept going, my fingers gliding to the apex of her thighs. Pushing aside her panties, I parted her slick folds.

"Why not?" I brushed my thumb over her clit, smiling. "You got something better to do?"

Her brows drew inward as she searched my face. "No. I just...I want..."

Anna wanted what I wanted.

To feel.

I slid my boxers over my hips as I continued to stroke her. A whimper escaped when I pulled away.

"Shh." Gripping the base of my shaft, I guided my tip to her entrance. "Is this what you want?"

Past the point of embarrassment, grief, or anything but need, Anna nodded. "Now...Sean...please."

Burying myself in her warmth, I stilled long enough to push her T-shirt up to reveal her perfect, pink nipples. Scoring my teeth over one stiff peak, I slammed into her again, deeper this time.

We were primal, unrestrained, and when her nails dug into my skin, a jolt of pure pleasure raced up my spine.

So fucking close.

But I didn't want this to end, didn't want to face the reality that waited outside this moment, so I rose to my knees and wrapped her legs around my waist. My fingers skimmed her breasts, her quivering belly, and finally the small strip of auburn hair between her legs.

"Let go for me, baby," I grunted, circling her tiny bud with my thumb. "I need you to come."

I needed to come. To spill all the pain and the loss and the emptiness coating my insides.

Anna's eyes rolled back and she gripped my arm.

"Sean!"

Her walls closed tight around me as she tipped over the edge, chanting my name like a mantra. Falling onto my elbows, I chased her to the bottom, meeting the end of her with one final thrust.

Anna cupped my cheek as the spasms rolled through me, and leaning into her touch, I pressed my lips to her palm.

"I love you, Anna-baby."

She twined her fingers into my hair, and guiding me to the crook of her neck, she whispered, "I love you too. Always."

MISSING FROM ME
order now!

ACKNOWLEDGMENTS

Jeff—Love of my life. All of my life. Words and music, baby.

Matthew and Victoria—The brightest stars in the night sky. My true north. I love you both.

Jim and Pat—Love you, mom and dad.

Peyton & Jacob—I love you more than you know, and more than I can say.

Bonnie Marie—Always in my thoughts. There's a little piece of you in everything I write. Love you.

And finally—to anyone who has touched my life, in big ways and small—*thank you*.

WHO IS JAYNE...

Jayne Frost, author of the Sixth Street Bands Romance Series, grew up with a dream of moving to Seattle to become a rock star. When the grunge thing didn't work out (she never even made it to the Washington border) Jayne set her sights on Austin, Texas. After quickly becoming immersed in the Sixth Street Music scene...and discovering she couldn't actually sing, Jayne decided to do the next best thing—write kick ass romances about hot rockstars and the women that steal their hearts.

Want to join the tour and become a Jayne Frost VIP?
Sign up for the **Sixth Street Heat Newsletter**
http://bit.ly/2fS3xiQ

STALK ME!

www.jaynefrost.com
jayne@jaynefrost.com

ALSO BY JAYNE FROST

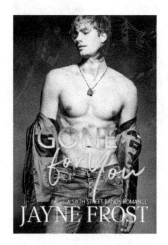

FREE EVERYWHERE

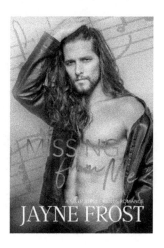

AVAILABLE NOW

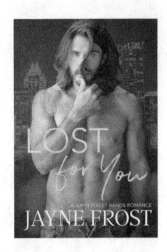

JANUARY 12th, 2018

CPSIA information can be obtained
at www.ICGtesting.com
Printed in the USA
BVHW040908050519
547383BV00016B/617/P